Also by Stephanie Ash

INSPIRATION

Musical Affairs

Stephanie Ash

**X
LIBRIS**

An *X Libris* Book

First published by X Libris in 1996

A CIP catalogue for this book
is available from the British Library.

ISBN 0 7515 1691 0

Photoset in North Wales by
Derek Doyle & Associates, Mold, Clwyd
Printed and bound in Great Britain by
Clays Ltd, St Ives plc

X Libris
A Division of
Little, Brown and Company (UK)
Brettenham House
Lancaster Place
London WC2E 7EN

Chapter One

JERRY ANSON LIKED to get surprises on his birthday. Well, thought Amelia, he certainly would be surprised when he woke up on this particular birthday. Very surprised indeed.

In fact, Jerry wasn't asleep at all. He was lying in bed, eyes half closed, listening to the sounds floating up from the kitchen. Crash, bang, shatter. Amelia boiling an egg. Jerry smiled slowly. She was useless in the kitchen. Fabulously beautiful, with the body of a goddess, but useless all the same. Which was why, he justified to himself, he hesitated over making an honest woman of her. And why he didn't feel too guilty about always keeping one eye open for someone new.

And that, unbeknownst to Jerry, was why Amelia was in the kitchen. Not, as Jerry thought, preparing him a sumptuous birthday breakfast but packing up her share of the kitchen crocks. There had been one blonde hair too many on her side of the bed.

Crash! She'd always hated that bloody novelty teapot.

Jerry pulled the duvet up to his chin and rolled over, unperturbed. He hoped Amelia had remembered that he'd recently given up taking sugar in his coffee.

Click. That was an incongruous sound in the breakfast repertoire. Slam. So was that.

An hour of silence passed before Jerry sat up in bed and allowed it to cross his mind that something might be wrong.

By which time Amelia was en route to a new flat and a new start in Kentish Town in Jerry Anson's own new car.

'Damn, damn, damn.'

Amelia stalled the jeep at the traffic lights for the second time in as many minutes. 'Why are there so many bloody sets of traffic lights in this damn town?' she asked no one in particular very loudly.

A middle-aged man in a white Porsche Carrera with the top down smiled up at the outburst. He gave the pretty red-haired driver of the Shogun what he assumed was a sexy wink. She gobbed her chewing gum out of her window and onto his passenger seat in reply.

'Oh no, not again!' Amelia cried. She could feel the tears welling up like an ocean behind her eyes. That was the exact same model of Porsche that Jerry had been driving when he took her on their first date ... The memory pricked her. Things were so different back then. He had opened the door of the car for her, taken her coat in the restaurant, pulled out her chair. So gentlemanly. So full of chivalry. Until he got what he wanted.

Amelia wiped her nose on the back of her hand.

'I'm not going to think about it,' she told herself.

She had held out for so long because she wanted to make sure that she was special to him. Not like all the other bimbos he met through his work.

Jerry Anson was a celebrated record producer. They had met at a music industry party. Amelia was there with an old friend, a gay pop singer, who was using her as a foil for the press. The headlines which appeared in the tabloids after that evening had been faintly amusing, Amelia remembered. Johnny had ended up punching Jerry and the tabloid press had reported that it was because Jerry had stolen Amelia, Johnny's beautiful mystery date, straight out from under his celebrated nose. Little did they know that the whole fracas had blown up because Jerry had insulted an inebriated Johnny's favourite orange Moschino tie.

In the circles in which Amelia had been moving at that time, relationships were based on strict theories of equity and exchange. At first glance, Jerry had seemed to Amelia to be about as attractive as an overweight bulldog chewing a wasp, but he wanted her and she wanted a record contract. He talked music, he talked production, he talked sessions. Even though they didn't turn out to be quite the sessions she had in mind.

But Amelia's initial pragmatism had been replaced by a very real lust. Like Titania in *A Midsummer Night's Dream*, she had emerged one evening from the ladies' room in Quaglino's or Le Café D'Amour (as they had romantically dubbed it), to see him chatting earnestly by candlelight into his mobile phone and fallen hopelessly in love. She couldn't explain it. Was it something to do with the soft wave of his hair, the square set of his jaw, the way his ears stuck out at 90 degrees . . .? Or the fact that he was talking to someone very big at Sony on her behalf . . .?

'For goodness sake, Amelia, he's so ugly!' she told herself vehemently, slamming her hands on the steering wheel. An elderly woman passing by on the pavement with her dog shrank back in surprise.

It was no use. It was hopeless. She was so deeply in love with that horrible little man, they would have to send Jacques Cousteau in after her.

As she wiped away her tears again she caught the lingering scent of Jerry's skin on her hand. His aftershave, his sweat, even his semen. It had been so hard to tear herself away from his side that morning. Even after her worst fears about his new PA had been confirmed by the blonde hair on her pillow and the naff silver earring under the sink. His hands could still mould her anxious mind as they caressed her agile body. His lips could still take any unhappy words straight out of her mouth with one tender, careful kiss . . .

But last night they had made love for the last time. The realisation stuck in Amelia's throat as she waited for the go-ahead at another set of lights and she gave out a strangled sob. She had let him nuzzle her soft pink breasts and draw a last path slowly up the inside of her thigh with his velvety tongue. He had pulled her close to him and entered her so slowly, so carefully, so reverently, that it was as if he too had grasped the finality of it all. With her shuddering orgasm, she had shed hot and salty tears. But he had settled into a deep sleep straight after without seeing those bitter teardrops at all.

She would never, never, never let herself become so enslaved by a faithless man again. He may have given her flowers, and he may have given her earth-shattering orgasms, but, Amelia reminded herself, Jerry Anson had never once given her a piece of his heart.

In his neat Victorian terraced house in Kentish Town, Richard Roberts paced the little sitting-room, setting straight the African knick-knacks and tossing unspeakable debris into the raffia wastepaper basket that stood by the door. The ad about his spare room had only gone into *Loot* the day before. The paper couldn't have been out for five minutes when he got the first call. A girl. Desperate, she sounded. She said she didn't care how big the room was, or how much he wanted for rent, as long as she had a bed and a piano. Ah yes, the piano. He'd put that in as a selling point and it had obviously worked, as a selling point that was . . . he wasn't sure about it's usefulness as a musical instrument.

Anyway, this girl had practically left him no choice. She was being made homeless, she said. She would have nowhere to go but the gutter if he didn't let her stay with him. What could he do when faced with such a dilemma? He told her she could move in the very next day. Richard glanced at his watch. She would arrive any minute now.

Amelia had said that she would pick up the keys from next door if he wasn't going to be in or up when she arrived, but Richard had called in sick so that he would be there to meet her. He was dying to see just what he had let himself in for. The feel-good factor of saving someone from a night on the streets had been replaced by a nagging question. Why did she have to leave her old flat so suddenly? He had a vision of a brutally murdered landlord on a brown carpeted floor. No, she didn't sound like an axe murderer. That was the worst case scenario. The best case was that she would turn out to be a complete stunner. Richard smoothed his thick dark hair down hopefully as he polished the mirror which stood on the mantelpiece.

Rat-tat-tat.

Richard swung the door open and in flew the

first of four suitcases.

'Give me a hand, will you?' shouted a vaguely familiar voice.

Richard trotted out to the Shogun, which was parked half on the pavement outside his house, and duly obliged the flame-haired siren who was slinging coats, vases and saucepans out of the passenger door and onto the pavement.

'That's it,' she announced, when Richard had been all but buried in a pile of cotton dhurry rugs.

Amelia slammed the car door and kicked it, hard. As Richard winced with that peculiar male automobile-empathy at the foot-shaped dent, she relieved him of a natural-coloured rough linen lampshade and marched into the house. There she collapsed, sobbing, onto the sofa.

Full of trepidation, Richard stretched out a welcoming hand.

'I'm Richard,' he said.

'Amelia,' she wailed in reply. Her shoulders continued to twitch up and down and she limply took his hand in hers. Her fingers were wet from wiping her face.

'I'm sorry,' she snorted into a handkerchief. 'I'm not normally like this, Richard. I promise.'

'Tea?' asked Richard suddenly. What else could one ask in such a situation, he thought.

Amelia nodded and Richard gratefully escaped his new housemate's company for the sanctuary of the kitchen.

From the kitchen door he had quite a good

view of the new girl. While the kettle boiled he sized her up. She was dabbing at her face with a scrunched up and fast disintegrating piece of pink tissue. Her eyes were red and piggy from crying. But on the whole, she looked OK. Richard definitely liked her coppery hair, which was unwinding itself from her kirby grips and falling in waves onto her black-clad shoulders. She was wearing black jeans and what looked like a black all-in-one that clung tightly to her slim arms. As she blew her running nose, Richard glimpsed her cleavage. Though she was slim, she wasn't at all flat-chested. A large pendant of amber hung like a golden tear between her breasts.

Richard found himself wishing he had made more of an effort with his appearance that morning.

'Milk?' he asked.

'Yes,' came the strangled reply, followed by the sound of a nose being blown.

'Sugar?' he asked.

'Yes. Two.'

He ladled them in with a cleanish-looking teaspoon. She had stopped crying now and was unfastening the latch on a square-shaped wicker basket. Richard stood with a cup in each hand, unwittingly awaiting the appearance of the second redhead to enter his life that day. Eliza the cat came hissing out of her box. Fat and grumpy and missing all her top teeth. She hadn't said anything about having a cat.

'She'd like a saucer of milk,' Amelia

announced. 'Not skimmed.'

Richard put down the steaming mugs and hurried back to the kitchen. A girl, a cat and a large quantity of those stripy Indian rugs he had always despised. Richard sneezed. Things around here, he thought, are about to change for good.

'Tell me about yourself,' Amelia had said before she promptly launched herself into her own life story. She was twenty-five, born in London to an English father and an American mother, now divorced. She had been educated in England, at a Gloucestershire convent school, but spent the summers with her mother in California. She'd been to college in the States too, before finally moving to England for good four years ago. That accounted for the strange accent she knew she had, she said. It was very slight and rather nice, Richard assured. She had two half-sisters from her father's first marriage, both older, both married, something which she would never be. Not after this last fiasco. She wrote songs which were a bit like Carpenters classics on the piano and wanted to play music for a living. She didn't have a day job but her wealthy parents still sent her 'guilt money' which would cover the rent.

The words became one long melodious stream of sounds in Richard's ears. Her face was less wet and blotchy now. The eyes, a watery blue, were fixed on the traffic-fume dirty window as she recounted a tale about her early life. Richard tried not to, but found he just couldn't stop his gaze

9

from wandering down from her face on a journey to her hips. From her hips, down her legs to her . . . it was then that he spotted it. On the floor next to one of her dainty lace-up boots. The unmistakable red and black wrapper of a Durex Arouser, ribbed.

'Ohmigod,' Richard breathed, barely audibly. His horrified eyes were transfixed. Had she noticed it too?

'And you, Richard,' she continued, oblivious to his sudden discomfort, 'do you have any brothers or sisters?'

'What?' He couldn't tear his gaze away from the embarrassing piece of foil on the floor.

'Do you have any brothers . . .?'

It was too late. Amelia's eyes had followed down his line of sight. She shifted her right foot slightly to see what it was hiding.

'Oh,' she blushed. She picked the wrapper up and tossed it into the raffia bin. 'My favourite sort.'

Richard gathered up the mugs and retired to the kitchen until he could breathe properly again. Ah well. At least she wouldn't think that he was some sad guy who never scored.

Her first night in her new home. Amelia felt cramped and cold in the narrow single bed, with Eliza the cat sleeping on her chest. She surveyed the unfamiliar surroundings. The Liechtenstein print her best friend had given her on that flowery wallpaper. It just didn't go. But Richard

10

had said that he would get round to doing this room up soon.

The piano mentioned in the advert stood against the far wall. It was a Victorian upright. With the original curly wooden legs still in place. Its lid was covered in piles of dusty old sheet music that she had yet to look through. She couldn't sleep. Amelia flicked on the bedside lamp and wandered across to her new piano. It was just a little different from Jerry's white baby grand . . . Tentatively, Amelia hit middle C and played a shaky chromatic scale. Not too far out of tune. She would have liked to have played more but Richard was probably sleeping. She had taken a peep into his room earlier and seen the double pine-framed bed. She remembered the condom wrapper. He must have a girlfriend, though he hadn't mentioned any names. He was a nice-looking guy, rugged even. Friendly. Tall. It would be a pity . . .

'No,' Amelia told herself, 'I have to live with the guy. You don't screw the crew.'

But as she settled down beneath the thin duvet, she couldn't stop herself from wondering what it might be like to unbutton his too-big jeans.

A picture came into her mind of Richard in the kitchen. Standing at the sink, washing their coffee mugs. His shirt half-tucked in, half-pulled out. Sleeves rolled up around strong and sinewy forearms. She would walk in behind him and silently slide her arms around his waist. He would be shocked, but say nothing, until her lips

11

lightly brushed the back of his neck, still golden brown from two weeks in the sun. He would quickly relax into the embrace. He's been thinking about this moment too. Can't resist her, doesn't want to.

Chapter Two

AMELIA WOKE, AS usual, just too soon, and no matter how hard she tried, shutting her eyes just would not bring back her happy dream. The sun was streaming in through the thin yellow curtains which hung at the long window. Amelia made a mental note to get those changed. It was seven a.m. and it was Saturday. What a bloody disaster!

Eliza had also awoken early and was pacing the unfamiliar room which had no cat flap. She was mewling fiercely. Amelia opened her bedroom door and booted the fat tabby out onto the landing.

Meanwhile Richard lay in bed on the other side of the wall, listening out for sounds of lodger life. He was strangely nervous about getting up, about wandering down into his own kitchen in his off-white dressing gown and dinosaur-feet slippers. He didn't look good in the morning. Bianca had told him. Bianca from Barbados. Owner of the Arouser found beneath the settee. Another one-week wonder of a relationship, that was. She was only too delighted to be with him until she found out that his record company job was in the accounts department. Oh sod her, Richard told himself. She may have had the legs of a baby giraffe but she had the voice of a chain-smoking wart-hog.

'Yeowwl!'

Someone from the room next door was up. Richard poked his tousled head around the door to investigate the unearthly howl and came face to face with Amelia. Overcome with guilt, she was poking her head out of her door to see what had become of the cat.

'Hello.' Her blush gave way to a wide smile. Though her eyes were still faintly pink, Richard could see that Amelia was generally the kind of person who looked great in the mornings. Their disembodied heads swapped pleasantries around the door frames for a while, then they agreed to emerge, more fully clothed, in five minutes' time and grab some breakfast in a nearby greasy spoon.

Richard ransacked his room in the search for a pair of clean underpants. It was like going on a date. There were no clean pants to be found. Oh, well. He remembered Murphy's Law. If he was wearing a pair of tatty Y-fronts, she would be bound to want to take his trousers off.

Amelia knocked at his door to let him know that she was done in the bathroom. She was dressed in a loose white cotton top with no sleeves and blue jeans. Most of her hair was scraped back from her face into an intricate plait. The amber pendant still hung around her neck. Richard found his eyes drawn to it as they talked. Amelia laughed nervously and folded her arms across her chest, feeling more than a frisson of pleasure at his obvious interest. On the way to the café, she linked her arm through his. It was warm outside already but the sweat which began to gather in the crook of Richard's elbow had little to do with the heat.

It was only a matter of time before Jerry missed his brand new Shogun. Probably longer than it would have taken the average guy, however, since he had a vague recollection of parking it outside Tramp on Thursday night and wasn't sure whether it had been stolen or he had just forgotten to drive it home. Amelia wouldn't have taken it, surely? He didn't think she even knew how to drive. When a sortie to Jermyn Street failed to come up with the wheels, he telephoned the police. They rang back quite quickly. They'd found his car. In Kentish Town.

'Kentish Town?' he said incredulously when the policeman let him know the address. He didn't know anyone there but he didn't like to request police back-up when he went to fetch it just in case the address turned out to be the vital clue to those missing hours on Thursday night.

He found the car easily, but didn't recognise

the house. He had just opened the Shogun's driver door and was climbing inside when a familiar voice screamed to him from a little way down the road.

'Stop, thief!' the redhead squealed. Jerry climbed back out of the car and waited on the pavement for Amelia to come hurtling up the road. She had just finished breakfasting and talking about her songwriting ambitions with Richard. He was following behind her. He had stopped at the shop on the corner to pick up some milk and twenty Silk Cut.

'Darling, what are you doing here?' Jerry asked warmly, arms outstretched.

'Don't you "darling" me,' said Amelia, wrestling the keys from his hand.

'What's going on? Where have you been? Who do we know in Kentish Town of all places?'

' "We" know nobody,' Amelia told him, spitting out the 'we' as if the word tasted bitter. 'I live here now.'

'What do you mean, you live here now?'

'I've left you, Jerry.'

'Left me? Don't be ridiculous. You haven't taken your curling tongs.'

'You can send them on. I've had enough of all your messing around. I know you're sleeping with that miserable little PA of yours. Well, I just hope she's good at shorthand . . .' Amelia accompanied her words with the most withering look she could muster when faced by the only man she had ever loved. Jerry's eyes narrowed.

16

She'd hit him straight on his Achilles' head, as it were.

'It was nothing, Amy.'

'And so are you, Jerry. Nothing but a part of my past. So, you can just take your stupid car – which keeps stalling anyway – and go.'

'Bunny, stop being a silly little girl and come back home with me. We can talk about this . . .'

He tangled loving fingers in her beautiful hair and fixed her watery eyes with his most penetrating gaze. Using her plaited hair as a line to reel her in he pulled her face towards his and parted his lips in readiness for a winning kiss.

'No,' she pulled herself away from his embrace unexpectedly. 'I can't. It's not just you who's found someone else, Jerry, I have too.' She looked desperately back down the street for her new housemate. 'His name is Richard.'

Richard was approaching them. Dawdling along, lighting up a cigarette as he walked. He had heard Amelia talking to someone as soon as he walked out the door of the shop and had heard the voices raised but decided to stay well out of it.

'Richard!' This time his name was being used as a command. Maybe she was really in trouble. Dropping his cigarette, Richard sprinted up the street like a knight in shining armour. Through the arch that Amelia's arm made with the car door, he could see a man, slightly shorter than she was. He was thick-set, clad in an expensive blue suit over a soft sage polo-neck jumper. He looked like an East End mafioso.

'Ah, Richard . . . meet Jerry, Jerry Anson, my ex. Jerry, this is Richard . . . my lover.'

Richard's face barely had time to register confusion before Amelia had fastened her lips to his and was forcing them apart with her tongue. His hands were raised in a gesture of bemusement and submission as her arms wrapped tightly around him and she kissed him frantically until they heard a vague 'Harrumph' and the sound of Jerry's smart leather-soled shoes beating a retreat. The door of the Shogun slammed shut, whereupon Amelia dropped Richard like a limpet letting go of its rock and fled back into the house. She collapsed on the sofa, sobbing, again.

Richard raised his fingers to his violently tingling lips and felt them for damage. Had that really just happened? Yes, he could taste lipstick. It had definitely happened. He watched the Shogun tear off into the traffic. So that was her 'ex'. Very flash.

Tentatively, Richard walked up to the front door and pushed it open. He crept over to where Amelia crouched and cried, sat down beside her and put an arm around her shoulders.

'So that was him?'

She nodded.

'He's a bit of a spud, isn't he?'

That line didn't succeed in stopping her tears, but it did drive Amelia further into Richard's arms. He felt the hot salt-water soaking through his clean cotton shirt and on to his chest. He squeezed her a little tighter to him and tenderly patted her slim back.

'Tea?' he asked, after he had been holding her for about ten minutes and felt that he was about to dissolve in her tears.

She nodded.

He pushed a piece of unused tissue between her fingers and left her to it.

Richard put the kettle on and then stood at the sink, looking out onto the weed-punctuated concrete that called itself the garden. He felt damp under the arms as well as all down the front of his shirt. He was still hot from the kiss on the doorstep. She was a strange girl. Incredible. Amazing. He didn't know whether to be angry or pleased. She had used him, hadn't she? But he supposed he had enjoyed it. He hadn't been kissed like that for months.

As he scanned the garden, he noticed that Eliza the cat was curled up in the tiny corner of the yard which was still in the morning sun. Amelia had brought that fleabag along without asking, he thought. Smeone who did that couldn't really have much regard for anybody else, or their feelings.

Amelia had got up from the sofa and stood at the kitchen door, unnoticed, watching Richard watching her cat. She liked the way his forearms looked in their rolled-up sleeves. His big, clean hands gripping the edge of the sink. His shoulders were broader than she had at first thought. Quietly she reached for her hair and began to unplait it, for effect.

'Don't turn around,' she begged Richard silently, as she crept up behind him and got almost close enough to stir the hair on his neck with her breath. She stretched out one hand and placed it on his hip, near his belt. He spun around in surprise and nearly knocked her over.

'Amelia, you nearly gave me a heart attack!'

'Don't worry, I'll make it better,' she told him, drawing herself level with his curious eyes. They widened involuntarily.

Now she was kissing him again, but this time, not because she wanted anybody to see.

Richard was frozen with shock at first but, as Amelia's soft lips wandered a little more gently over his face, he let his hands rest lightly on her shoulders. She brought her fingers up to cup his square, stubbly chin.

'Amelia, are you sure . . .?' Richard began to ask a question when she broke away from him briefly to get some air.

'Ssssh,' she replied, silencing him with a finger on his burning lips.

Richard leant back heavily against the aluminium sink and let himself be swept up in the moment.

His tongue pushed its way between her lips and began to explore her straight, white teeth. She stopped moving her mouth for a moment, just opened it a little wider and let him inside. He ran his tongue along the inside of her upper lip.

Tickling her. A satisfied sigh escaped her when he moved his attention to another part of her face.

Richard placed a kiss on each of her closed eyelids, which fluttered as he pulled away from them. Her mouth was curved into a contented smile.

'Amelia.'

He pushed her hair away from her face and kissed her exposed white forehead. Then he let his lips touch her alabaster cheeks, which were growing a little pinker now. She tilted her head back so that her lips were in the line of fire again. Her hands curled purposefully around his neck, then she slid them down, exploring his upper body, squeezing the muscles that she had imagined lay beneath the cool cotton chambray when they first met a day before. Her fingers found the front of his shirt. And the buttons.

'Amelia, do you think we . . .?'

She cut him dead with a kiss. He acquiesced to the hands which had now breached his shirt and roamed predatorily over his pleasantly hairy pecs. Still surprised by the whole chain of events, Richard hesitated to follow her lead, his hands still motionless on her shoulders while she delicately rolled one of his small, hard, nipples between her forefinger and thumb. He wanted to close his eyes and relax but before he could do that he had to believe that she wasn't going to wake up and stop kissing him any second now.

'You can join in if you like,' she told him pointedly.

Richard squeezed her shoulder blades and allowed himself to feel his way down her spine to where her soft jersey top was tucked into her jeans. There were no fastenings to be undone, so he merely untucked it and let his hands slip underneath. She shivered and stiffened at the coolness of his fingers against her back, but the chill was gone in a moment and she relaxed her body against him once more, her pink cheek against his bare chest, pressing herself into him like a cat.

She was wearing no bra, Richard discovered as he reached her shoulder blades without any obstruction. Her hands were now on his buttocks, pulling him away from the sink and closer to her. He lifted the jersey top up and out of the way so that they finally stood bare chest to chest.

Uncomfortable with the material bunched up like that above her breasts, Amelia let Richard go briefly and hurriedly stripped the vest right off. Richard couldn't stop himself from giving a little exclamation of pleasure upon seeing her white breasts with their pinky nipples, framing the amber teardrop that felt cold when it touched his skin. After allowing him just a few seconds of contemplation, Amelia reached up behind him to the bright yellow Venetian blind that hung at the kitchen window and pulled it quickly shut.

'This is it,' Richard thought. The future, or what was going to happen in the next hour at the very least, suddenly became blindingly clear.

In the semi-darkness, Amelia took hold of his

hand and led him out of the kitchen, through the sitting-room and up the creaky stairs. Richard followed willingly, wanting to say something, ask her if this was really happening, but afraid that if he did so the spell would be broken. They passed her room and went straight into his. Amelia had already ascertained that the bed in there was bigger than her own. Richard's untidy room smelt musty and warm, unaired, like a cocoon. Dust stirred in the narrow shaft of sunlight that pushed in through a chink in his heavy mustard velvet curtains.

Amelia backed herself up to the edge of the bed, let her knees fold and flopped backwards onto it. Richard stood in front of her, quickly stripping off his unbuttoned shirt. Amelia almost swam backwards up the bed, pushing aside the brightly coloured duvet and the pillow so that soon there was nothing on the mattress but her and the fitted sheet. She was fiddling with the flies of her jeans. She raised one foot at a time so that Richard could grab each denim leg and help her tug it off. Soon she was clad only in a pair of black jersey and Lycra panties that fitted perfectly the gentle curve of her hips. She parted her legs suggestively and writhed a little with her hands above her head. Richard was going to have to take off his own trousers. Amelia couldn't help smiling as she watched him hop from foot to foot in his hurry to get to her side, and then at the Mickey Mouse boxer shorts which he had put on that morning without expecting anyone else to see them. The curse of the dreadful underpants had struck once again.

Richard knelt on the bed between Amelia's casually parted legs. She hooked her thumbs into the elastic of his funny shorts and tugged them down unceremoniously. Then she took hold of her own pants and began to do the same, bringing her legs up around Richard's body and together to get the black Lycra off.

Richard fell onto the naked body before him, peppering her breasts and torso with kisses like a traveller falling upon water in the desert. She squirmed delightedly as his hands explored every inch of her, massaging her long, slender thighs, caressing her delicately rounded stomach. She trembled as he bent to kiss the spot where her left leg flowed smoothly into her body, her most sensitive point, sending arrows of delight up to her head. She prayed that he would find it again soon as his mouth travelled upwards to her waist and followed the curve of her body as far as her arm.

Suddenly she took hold of him, more forcibly than he had ever imagined, and pulled him down so that he lay flat on top of her, his straight, firm penis nestling between her thighs. Amelia sought out his mouth again and kissed him hard, her hands clenching his buttocks rhythmically at the same time. One of his hands had insinuated its way between them and was beginning to caress her aching mons, searching for a way into her.

'Penetrate me with your fingers,' she whispered urgently.

Richard gulped but did as he was asked. As his middle finger slipped between her labia and found her already wet and slippery, she sighed audibly as though he had taken a pin to an inflatable dinghy.

'That feels good,' she said when Richard began to move the finger slowly around, in and out. He smiled with the thought that he was giving her pleasure. A pleasure which was as much his as hers. As he rolled back so that he was on his side with his fingers still in her, his cock rested for a moment on her hip. He felt harder than he had ever done. Ready to come in great gushing spurts without her even laying her little finger on him. She bucked her hips in excitement so that her flesh brushed against his balls. He let out a sudden gasp that made her open her eyes and look at him questioningly.

'I feel like I'm going to burst,' he said apologetically.

'So do I,' she said. 'Let's not waste it.'

Within seconds she had manoeuvred herself so that she was now astride Richard, who lay flat on his back. He looked up at her in shock and amazement. No one had ever taken control like this before. She was holding his penis in her hand, getting him into position beneath her. Tiny moans and squeaks of excitement escaped her pretty mouth as she began to move down and his purple glans touched her wet and ready pussy. She teased them both for a moment by rubbing the smooth head back and forth across her labia like a lipstick until the anticipation became too much for either him or her to bear. Then she used the fingers of one hand to open herself a little more and . . . suddenly she pushed herself down.

Amelia groaned in ecstasy at the sensation of being filled by his glorious dick. It went in to the hilt straight away, so that his balls touched her buttocks. The feeling of being entered so deeply and so perfectly with that first thrust made her giddy with delight.

Having savoured that first moment she put her hands on Richard's shoulders and readied herself to bring some movement into the act. Slowly she drew her backside up so that he began to slip away from her. All the way up so that only the very top of his penis still remained within. Richard burned with joy. He felt as if a host of tiny tongues were licking him all the way up the length of his shuddering shaft to the tip. His hands groped blindly for her thighs so that he could pull her back down onto him again.

But Amelia drove back down of her own accord soon enough, welcoming the invasion of his penis into her body like the waves of the tide rushing back into the shore. She felt so wonderfully wanton, with the shaft of sun cutting across her breasts and his willing body beneath her thighs. She closed her eyes and threw her head back in rapture as she worked her thighs slowly then gradually increased the pace.

Richard had given in to the sensation. He was no longer trying to hold back. Each time her body swept down to meet his, he raised his own hips and gripped her tightly to him. His stomach tensed. He could feel his balls stirring, his shaft stiffening to the point where it hardly seemed like part of his flesh at all. He strained upwards to meet her glistening mouth for another kiss.

'Come, come, come,' Amelia was chanting in a half human, half animal voice. She was moving up and down like a crazed machine, her face changing as the crisis approached. Her climax was gathering within her like a storm cloud of lust. 'Oh, please, come now,' she whispered. 'Come now, Richard. Please come now.'

'Yes, yes, yes!' Richard's grip on her thighs tightened, his fingers turning her skin white with their pressure. His face twisted. His eyes screwed shut. He was gritting his teeth as though to get to his climax he would have to break through a brick wall.

But get there he did.

The force of Richard's orgasm could have shot Amelia straight off the bed. He let forth an incredible roar as his loins pumped furiously beneath her. She was calling out too, her fingers digging hard into his sweat-covered shoulders. The muscular walls of her vagina were matching his rhythm, pumping him dry. As the waves reached their maximum intensity, they pushed their bodies together as though they were trying to make them one for all time. Amelia threw back her head and clutched at handfuls of her hair. Richard exploded into her. Finally, completely, losing all semblance of control.

As her vagina was flooded and overflowing with the mingled secretions of their passion, Amelia collapsed onto Richard and clung to him while the crisis of their climax passed, laughing and crying all at the same time.

Afterwards, as Amelia dozed in the heavy atmosphere of Richard's room, he ran a slow hand through her long hair and replayed the scene which had just taken place through his buzzing mind. For now he was a very happy man indeed but already he had the nagging thought that he was going to be able to repent this particularly amazing event at his leisure.

Chapter Three

'I'VE GOT A GIG!'

Amelia bounced into the kitchen where Richard was making toast. She had been living in Kentish Town for a week now and seemed much happier than when she had first arrived. She had made a effort to make herself known to the local landlords and promoters as a singer/songwriter and already it had paid off.

'That was Lawrence Willow on the phone. One of the acts for Thursday night has pulled out and he wants me to take their place. Me! It's at the Bull and Gate.'

'Great, that's just round the corner,' said Richard. 'I'll be there.'

'Er, well.' Amelia shifted from foot to foot. 'I'd rather you weren't, actually, Richard. It's just that having someone I know sitting in the audience always makes me feel a little bit on edge . . . And apparently there are going to be a couple of A & R men, talent-spotters, in the audience to see the headlining act, so I'd like to play as well as I possibly can. Could be my big break,' she added with a sorry smile.

'Okay.' Richard tried to hide his disappointment. 'I'll stay away. I'm sure you'll knock 'em dead anyway.'

'Do you think so?'

'Of course I do.'

'Really, really?'

'Yes, really. I've heard you practising. Your new songs sound great. Like Tori Amos.'

Amelia's eyes narrowed.

'Okay, not like Tori Amos,' said Richard, back-pedalling. 'Better. You will blow their socks off. I only wish I could see you do it.'

Amelia was smiling broadly. 'When I play Wembley Arena, I promise you'll be in the very front row.' She flung her arms around Richard's neck and let him twirl her around with her feet off the floor. 'Thursday night. I'm so excited,' she told him. Then she squealed. 'That's tomorrow. What on earth am I going to wear?'

Richard watched her retreating figure and felt a faint twang, like Cupid's bow snapping, in his chest. Since their surprising encounter on Saturday, they had not slept together again. In fact nothing had even been said about the incident. But she had been very affectionate, he supposed. Hugging him and kissing him, though just a little too fraternally for his liking. Richard had decided not to push it. They had known each other for just a week or so. Amelia was probably still smarting over that snake of an ex-boyfriend. Richard had all the time in the world, and he was sure his time would come again.

Jamie Nettles liked to think he was as 'dangerous' as his namesake. Dressed in the softest black leather jeans, with no underpants beneath to spoil the line, and a Byronesque white shirt, he waltzed into the dingy pub chatting animatedly on his mobile phone. He was fashionably late, as usual. The gig he was due to watch had started an hour earlier. The manager of the first of the three acts glared across at the errant A & R man, who was widely known to be the most asinine and arrogant but also, unfortunately, one of the most important and influential in the business.

'Awright, Dave?' Jamie nodded to the balding man. The group the bald guy managed had a modicum of talent but were too ugly to be of any interest to this particular impresario. No, Jamie was there to see the act that was on next. Girl singer. Half American, or something. Lawrence thought she had some style and was a bit of a babe, to boot. Jamie wondered whether, coming from Lawrence, that was really a recommendation.

'Drink, Jamie?'

A shadowy figure had appeared at his side. A girl with a complexion the colour of the powder she used up her nose, a centre parting and a smoker's cough. It was Marilyn, his constant companion and sometime lover. She was hanging around with Jamie because she wanted a record deal, and his babies, in that order. Jamie was with her because, while she was an appalling guitarist, she could always manage to get some good gear.

'D'you park the car okay?' he asked her.

'Yeah,' she drawled.

'Good.' Jamie hated parking cars. That was his only problem. The more successful he was, the bigger his company car, and the harder it became for him to park.

The death metal act on stage finished their encore to a round of polite applause from the assembled girlfriends in the audience. Jamie winced at the final ear-splitting chord and mused that it might be worth signing them up just to be able to ensure that they spent the next two years in a soundproof room. While his companion rolled another cigarette and the next act's gear was shifted onstage, Jamie scanned the dingy bar. He recognised a couple of faces. The new exec from EMI. Interested in Death Metal? That was a surprise. Lawrence, the no-hoper guy who promoted the gigs in this godawful place. No girls worth speaking of. This singer had better be good. There was nothing Jamie liked less than to spend an hour in a place where no one was worthy of his decorative presence. He leant on the bar and gazed at his reflection in the glass behind the optics as he rearranged a bright-blond wave over one eye. Not the trendiest of haircuts, as his prodigy bands often teased him, but the girls all loved it. His wraithlike friend nudged his arm and motioned the suggestion of another pint. He mimed a half over the sound of the next act setting up. He had to drive home.

Amelia trod nervously onto the stage. The previous acts had been ten times heavier than her and she was sure that at the first sight of her, with her elegant high-waisted black dress and pre-Raphaelite hair, the place would clear.

She sat down at the keyboards and cleared her throat.

'It's another bloody Tori Amos.' Jamie's companion affected boredom and checked his eyes worriedly for the favourable reaction she knew this pretty redhead would get. He hadn't heard her comment. He tucked his mobile phone tightly into his back pocket and moved closer to the stage.

Her voice trembling with nerves, Amelia announced her first song. Richard's words played through her mind. He had faith in her. He had sat up half the night with her telling her so. She was going to do just fine. She almost wished she hadn't told him not to come. Wished that she could look out into the dark hall and see a friendly face amongst the strangers.

'Heartbreaks and promises,' she announced quaveringly and began to play, hitting the first few notes of her newest song perfectly. She smiled and heaved a sigh of relief as she entered the first chorus. Her stage fright was gone, banished. It was all plain sailing from now on.

Jamie Nettles folded his arms and leaned back against a nicotine-stained pillar. He wasn't sure if the girl was good, but she was damn well gorgeous. So, he figured, he might as well reserve judgement until she'd finished her set and he had her safely en route to his bed.

'You were great,' said Jamie, flashing the girl what he hoped was a warm smile.

'Oh, thanks.' Amelia was still shaking slightly with nerves. Her chosen career was going to be a lot harder than she had ever imagined. 'I'm glad you liked it.'

'I'm Jamie Nettles.' He held out his hand. 'Gallagher Records. A & R.' He fetched out a business card from his back pocket and twirled it between his fingers before giving it to her. He had practised that move. Amelia's eyes flashed excitedly. 'Did you write those songs yourself?'

She nodded eagerly, reading his card. 'I did, yes. All of them. Gallagher Records,' she murmured. That label sounded familiar.

The final act struck up their first song and the room was filled with discord. Jamie asked Amelia another question, which went unheard above the noise, then used the opportunity to take her aside by the arm and whisper straight into her pretty little ear.

'Want to go someplace quiet to talk about your act?' he asked.

34

'OK,' Amelia agreed, giving him a quick up-and-down glance while he flicked back his hair. 'Lead the way.' Jamie sashayed on ahead of her. He had a beautiful ass.

Jamie whooshed Amelia straight past Marilyn, who dropped her half-finished roll-up in disbelief. He hoped she hadn't left any of her rubbish in his car. Outside, Jamie motioned the beautiful redhead towards his sleek black roadster. She raised an eyebrow approvingly but seconds before she got in, he noticed that it was clamped.

'That can wait until tomorrow,' he said casually, stepping out into the road to hail them both a taxi. He was secretly relieved that he wouldn't have to unpark. 'What do you want to eat?' he asked. 'Chinese, Japanese, Italian?'

Over chimichanga and tacos at a Mexican place on Upper Street, Jamie set to work.

'And then I signed "Stegosaurus" . . .' Amelia nodded politely between mouthfuls of her spicy rice as Jamie ran through his long and successful repertoire of bands. They were mostly heavy rock, which made her wonder why he was interested in her. But hey, this meal was on his company expenses. Jamie reached for the wine-bottle that stood between them and somehow contrived to touch her hand when asking her if she wanted a top-up. The butterfly of first lust beat its wings briefly against the walls of her chest.

'What was that last band you mentioned?' she asked, regaining her composure.

'Stegosaurus,' he replied.

'Oh, yeah,' said Amelia, 'I think I've heard of them.' She hadn't.

'They went top twenty with their third single on Sunday. It's called "I wanna be your underwear." Inspired, eh?' Jamie ran a hand through his hair. He'd be upgrading his car again if they had just one more hit. What a headache.

Amelia felt good. It suddenly struck her that she hadn't really thought about Jerry at all that day and even remembering that she hadn't thought about him didn't dampen the happy mood which was building inside her. She was in a restaurant, eating good food, drinking great wine with a guy who appreciated her music, and had the looks of an apprentice Greek god to boot. And this Greek god definitely seemed to fancy her back. Why else did his every move result in brushing her hand, or her knee beneath the table?

'More wine?' he asked again. She hadn't touched her glass since the last time he asked. He was nervous. She had him on the run. Amelia placed her hand lightly over the top of her glass in refusal.

'Let's get a coffee, yeah? And then I really ought to be going to bed,' she told him. Jamie smiled, acknowledging the undercurrent which made her say 'to bed' rather than 'home'.

'I guess that at this point there's only one thing

36

left to say,' Jamie said as the taxi hovered outside Amelia's door. 'Your place or mine?'

His place, she decided, and the taxi set off again. Amelia wasn't quite sure why, but she had been distinctly uneasy about taking Jamie back to her own house. At least if she was at his place she could be the one to take the initiative and leave when she wanted to.

Jamie's first-floor flat in Camden was sparsely decorated. It was painted cream throughout. The floors were of pale polished wood, studded here and there with brilliant woollen rugs. An intriguing blue-green painting of nothing in particular hung above the fireplace. Amelia wasn't sure whether it was the flat of someone with immensely good taste or just someone who hadn't bothered to do anything much to it since he moved in. Her host flicked a switch and the room was suddenly filled with a subtle pink light which emanated from a peculiar-looking lamp on a three-legged table beside the sofa.

Jamie emerged from the kitchen with two glasses of brandy. No, not brandy, he told her, Calvados. Ah yes, she nodded, savouring the vague scent of apples before she took a sip and seriously burned her throat. Jamie slumped back on to the king-size sofa beside her. His Cuban-heeled cowboy boots had gone and his feet were bare. Amelia, who for some reason was always acutely aware of people's feet, decided that his were nice. Long, narrow and brown. Nails nicely trimmed and no hairy toes. Jamie drew one leg up so that his foot rested on the edge of the sofa and studied her shy-looking figure from his position of carefully assumed indolence.

'Comfortable?' he asked.

Amelia suppressed a nervous giggle. She kicked off her own shoes and drew both her feet up onto the sofa between them.

'I am now,' she told him.

Jamie rested his wrist on the upraised knee so that his glass dangled just in front of his shin. Amelia fixed her eyes on the swirling contents to avoid the scrutiny of his gaze. She took another sip from her own glass, barely letting any of the vile-tasting liquid into her mouth. Her lips tingled hotly, and she was sure that he would be able to see them growing a deeper red as bad thoughts began to creep into her mind. Prickles of anticipation ran along the back of her neck and down her spine. She could sense him shifting. The inevitable approaching. Suddenly he changed position, put his glass on the floor, took her glass from her hot little hand and pushed her backwards onto the sofa, his entire body touching hers at the same time as his lips as they both sank heavily into the soft cushions.

'I'm sorry,' he said insincerely as he came up for air. 'I just had to do that.'

Amelia feigned surprise. It was always best to let the guy think that it was his idea, that things were proceeding at his chosen pace. Jamie looked beautifully dishevelled now. The second and third buttons of his shirt had mysteriously come undone and revealed a light covering of hair on his chest. A discreet gold chain from which dangled a simple crucifix nestled between his pecs. It moved with him, sliding over his collar bones as he repositioned himself at her side. His hand cupped the side of her face, her chin resting on its heel.

'You can do it again if you like,' she told him softly.

Jamie needed no more encouragement. He brought her face close to his and plunged his tongue between her happily parted lips. The air was forced out of her body by his ardent embrace. She breathed in through her nose, relishing the smell of his aftershave, which warmed each intake of oxygen with amber and other exotic spices. She let her hands settle on his broad, thinly covered back and moved them over the fine cotton, feeling the powerful lineation of his muscles. Here was a man who definitely worked out.

He was making soft mewling sounds and his touch, after that first clumsy attempt, was surprisingly soft and tender. He pulled away from her occasionally, his face cut across by a broad smile, almost as if he was checking that he still had her full and rapt attention. His hands flattened out on her shoulder blades, then he slid them up and down, bringing blood rushing to her cheeks in anticipation as he found the tiny button that fastened her dress at the nape.

He fumbled the button open but the slit which such an action revealed was barely big enough for his hand. He contented himself for a moment with a small foray across her chilly shoulders with his well-kept fingers. Then he found her bra strap, followed it a little way down but soon realised that he just couldn't get to anything this way.

Amelia meanwhile was dealing with the remaining fastenings on his shirt. They popped apart easily and soon the shirt was open to the waist. She pulled away from his kiss and looked down at his exposed torso. He was lean. The muscles on his abdomen showed clearly, highlighted by a covering of dark hair that ran in a line from his belly button and disappeared beyond the belt of his leather jeans. Amelia's hands grasped the tops of his thighs as she returned to the kiss. The leather of his expensive jeans was so soft that she felt as though she was already touching his skin. She shifted position until her long skirt was no longer trapped beneath her and Jamie could lift the whole black dress over her head and out of the way.

She heard him draw breath in approval when he saw what the unveiling had revealed. Amelia let her head fall back so that her long red hair tumbled around her bare shoulders. Her perfectly rounded breasts bounced proudly up like twin suns from an intricately lacy bra. She was wearing exquisitely delicate knickers and beneath them, a suspender belt to match. Even her fine black stockings had lacy tops to them. She always like to dress for all possible eventualities and was very pleased now, knowing that an eventuality had popped up and Jamie was about to become as malleable as a soft dick in her warm hand.

When she felt that he had had sufficient opportunity to take the vision in, she returned to the business of setting him free from his own clothes. The voluminous white shirt slipped easily back from his shoulders. Amelia quickly tugged it free from his leather pants and tossed it aside. It billowed in the air like a sail as it fell to the floor.

Now for his belt.

Her fingers found their way to the heavy silver buckle. Jamie only looked down at the hands which were undressing him and gave a tiny, strangled noise of approval. Amelia had gathered from a brief exploration of his buttocks while they were kissing that he was not wearing any underpants and, since the fine black leather was the last barrier between her hands and his total nudity, she wanted this particular moment to last.

The free end of the belt was loosened. Amelia slid the long leather strip out from the loops. The feeling of his belt slipping away from around his waist provoked another of Jamie's peculiar little mews. Once she had pulled it completely free, Amelia took the redundant belt in both hands and looped it carefully around his strong neck, using it like a lasso to pull him to her. His eyes were closed. Amelia noticed with pleasure that his dark brown eyelashes were long enough to brush against his cheeks. She couldn't resist rubbing her nose softly against his. His hands blindly sought her warm breasts in their lacy confines.

Amelia slowly undid one of the tight silver buttons on his trousers while Jamie deftly unclipped her bra with one hand as though he had been born for the special purpose of doing so. She exhaled in pleasure at the sensation of her heavy breasts suddenly swinging free, their nipples already hard and ready to gratefully receive his urgent kiss.

Pop went another of Jamie's buttons. The line of hair which originated at his belly button became altogether more prolific here beneath his waistband. Amelia ran a teasing finger through the tawny curls. His smooth penis, still held down by the tightness of his flies, seemed to be straining upwards. Jamie's fingers played along the hem of her close-fitting panties, slipping under the elastic until his hands were cupping the twin cheeks. At the same time his mouth fluttered down her throat to her shoulder. He was breathing heavily as she let the final fly buttons go. Amelia was sure that her entire body would be flushed and pink by now. The Spartan sitting-room, which had been slightly cold when they first came in was suddenly starting to feel very warm indeed.

Jamie got up from the sofa and stood before her so that finally she could more easily pull his body-hugging trousers down. His dick sprang free and stood straight out in front of him, level with her eyes.

'It's rude to point,' Amelia laughed.

Coquettishly, she lifted her hair up away from her neck with both hands and held it on top of her head while she took in the picture of Jamie in his naked glory. Jamie looked at her, then at his dick. At her red mouth, then at his dick. The invitation was only too clear.

Amelia let her hair drop back onto her shoulders and shuffled forwards to the edge of the sofa. Jamie got into position between her stockinged legs. Amelia wrapped a hand around each of his thighs and pulled him closer still, her mouth widening into a tantalising smile as she let the pinky-purple glans bob up and down, up and down, just millimetres away from her slick glossy lips. Jamie placed his palms on her shoulders. He could hardly believe his luck. Not only was she gorgeous, but she actually looked as if she wanted to do this. Gently, he pulled her towards him so that she had to open her mouth to let him inside. Teasingly, she pulled away again once more.

'Tell me if I get it wrong,' she told him with the earnestness of someone taking their first driving lesson.

'I'm sure you won't,' he replied calmly, while his body screamed at her to hurry up.

Amelia ran a provocative fingertip along the gully where his abdomen joined his leg. A soft chuckle escaped her lips. There was nothing submissive about this position for her. He was putty in her hands, about to become marble between her teeth. Her lips formed a perfect 'O' as she zeroed in.

'Mmmmm.' A sigh like escaping steam flowed from Jamie's mouth. The moment her lips had closed oh so gently on his purple head, he had taken her red head in his hands. As her tongue worked diligently around the tip, he scrunched up great handfuls of her hair, even rubbing some of it against his downy stomach. Amelia wasn't a deep throater. She liked to use her hands and tongue, gently massaging the foreskin up and down the shaft with her fingers while her tongue flickered across the smooth glans and sensitive raphe. She closed her eyes and savoured the taste of his clean penis, growing saltier with semen as she licked him, and listened eagerly for the sighs which let her know that she was doing it right. She worked all over the shaft with her tongue, and right down to his balls. Jamie's hands were going mad in her hair, twisting and pulling harder than he knew, but Amelia bore his clumsiness for now, guessing that it was a sign of deep, deep appreciation.

Letting his glans drag slowly out over her bottom lip, Amelia moved her attention to his balls. She blew on the hairy sacs which hung swollen and pulsing between his hard thighs. The skin on Jamie's balls moved in reaction like a covering of molten lava. Eventually Amelia cupped one in each hand and fondled them like two precious golden spheres while she licked sporadically at the bobbing glans. He was getting really hot now. She would have to use one hand to hold the shaft still while she licked at it.

'Amelia . . .' He breathed her name as though it were a word in a foreign language. His fingers tightened in her hair. 'Slow down, slow down, please. I feel like I'm going to burst. You are driving me mad . . .'

Reluctantly unfastening her tingling hands from his shaft, he pulled her up from the sofa so that they were face to face again. He had to stop her or he would be useless for the rest of the night. He kissed her again, her mouth salty with his own semen.

Amelia was still wearing her knickers. Jamie gave them a yank and they quickly joined the rest of her clothes on the floor. He didn't want her to take off her stockings and suspenders, not yet.

'You've got such a warm pussy,' he told her as he placed his right hand purposefully between the tops of her legs. Normally, she would have shuddered at such a description but somehow, that night, coming from him, it seemed right. His fingers brushed across her fast-awakening labia towards her tingling clitoris. It was her turn to tremble now.

'Is it as warm right inside?' he asked.

Unconsciously, Amelia spread her legs a little further apart and raised herself on tiptoe to make it easier for him to find out.

She sighed with a delirious mixture of pleasure and relief as the first finger slipped easily inside.

45

She was feeling so wet. So very hot. She ground her silky mons against his welcome hand, begging him without words to find her clitoris and fast. Jamie quickly picked up on her subconscious signal and was soon there. Amelia let out a shaking breath as she felt her newly-discovered clitoris begin to stiffen and grow large.

'Faster,' she murmured. Jamie obliged. Amelia's legs shook and became unsteady as the pleasure became more intense and she had to get him to let her collapse back down onto the bed-sized sofa again. He tumbled on top of her, still working his hand furiously in her body as though he was revving up the engine of a sleek red car. He thought that her face, in the throes of her lust, was even more beautiful than it had looked at the club and in the restaurant. Her darkening eyes had taken on a feline quality, seeming almost to draw out his soul, as she looked at him from beneath lowered lids.

'And harder,' she whispered.

Jamie's excitement grew in line with hers. He reared away from her and his dick waved between them like an excited spectator watching the big match. His feet slid backwards on the shiny wooden floor as he tried to put even more power behind his arm.

'More! More!' Amelia's breathing was getting so heavy now that Jamie could hardly hear her words. Her hands fumbled for his penis. No matter how many fingers he put inside her, it

46

seemed that they would never be enough to satisfy her desperation. Her eyes greedily took in his dick. Hard and straight. Big enough to make a difference. Amelia twisted around so that her legs fell off the sofa, her bottom at the edge. She opened her knees. Jamie dropped to his knees between them, still working her clitoris like a demon with his love-slick fingers.

'Fuck me, Jamie,' she hissed with a voice that was barely her own. She pushed his hands out of the way and placed her own fingers on her labia, pulling them apart so that the entrance to her vagina was explicitly clear. Jamie pulled himself into position, steadying himself with his hands on her creamy thighs. Her vagina was at the perfect height. Holding his dick in his hand like a weapon, he penetrated her. Her hands clutched at the loose soft cushions behind her head. Her arousal-pink face first registered a fleeting look of shock at the strength of his thrust, then pleasure, her eyebrows raised.

Open-mouthed with ecstasy, Jamie slowly drew back his hips and pulled his shaft a little way clear of its deep warm haven. Amelia groaned as her swollen lips vibrated softly with his passing and she grabbed for his waist to stop him from withdrawing too far. Jamie looked momentarily as if he were about to speak but was unable to find the words. Amelia used the sides of his slim waist to lever him back inside until his pelvis grazed her clitoris and his balls slapped against the cheeks of her bottom. Jamie's hands rested, one on each of her breasts, while he savoured the feeling of the muscles in her hot narrow pussy with which Amelia was holding on tightly to his shaft.

Amelia was sliding off the sofa. Gradually both she and Jamie slipped to the floor, still fastened together. Amelia groped for a cushion which she knew had fallen off the sofa earlier and wiggled it in beneath the small of her back. Her hips were raised to the perfect angle now. Jamie was as deep within her as it was possible for a man to go. He felt her hands take possession of his buttocks, kneading them, encouraging him to begin pumping again now that she was comfortable beneath him. Jamie raised himself on his arms so that their bodies were joined only at the pelvis. Amelia gazed in tacit approval at the taut tensed arms which held Jamie above her, then she looked down along her body to where his semen-shiny shaft was slowly gliding in and out.

The combination of the friction of Jamie's movements and the sight of them taking place were almost instantly too much. Amelia felt a spasm in her vagina, pushing a sigh from her mouth. She raised her knees and placed her feet flat on the floor for leverage. Her thighs were trembling with a sensation of melting as she brought them in tightly against Jamie's waist.

She longed to force him to speed up, to thrust into her as though he was trying to thrust through her, but Jamie was taking things at his own measured pace, using his shaft as an instrument of slow torturous pleasure, determined that he would not be the first to let go. Amelia's head rolled slowly from one side to another. Her eyes were closed now, her eyebrows knitted together. She was biting her lower lip. Around his waist, her thighs gripped harder and harder. Her hands on his buttocks were trying to flatten him into her.

'Aaaaah!' A cry she just couldn't hold inside told him that she was nearly there. For Jamie too, the restraint was at last becoming too much to bear. Like a stallion spurred on by the crack of the whip, he finally agreed to let her hands set the pace. Her pelvis rose frantically up to meet his. Their bodies crashed together as they raced towards the finish. He had collapsed down onto her now, his mouth at her ear. The sound of his panting, his passionately uncontrolled exhalations was arousing her still more.

Suddenly, Amelia felt as though she was a mighty river, rushing through a narrowing tunnel, the pressure building up until there was no option but to burst open the walls which were channelling her inwards. She lost her rhythm, could no longer keep up. Jamie carried on, his face changed above her, barely recognisable in his ecstasy. Amelia's hips no longer moved in time with his but pushed ever upwards as she was ripped apart by the first wave of her climax, to be joined, fractions of a second later, by his.

Like a single frozen frame of an all-action film, their bodies were still momentarily, pressed together and held there by the forces which still raged inside them. Amelia counted the tiny grunts which accompanied each spasm of her lover's thunderous orgasm, while hers rolled continuously, relentlessly, like the angry sea breaking through a dam.

When the crisis was over, they stayed locked together on the floor, neither wanting to be the first to pull away from the other's body. Jamie's softening penis still felt caressed from time to time by Amelia's pulsating vaginal walls. But soon she found she was growing cold, so Jamie pulled a throw off the sofa and laid it over the top of them both. They stayed there on the floor until the throw and the pink light could keep them warm no more.

Chapter Four

'NICE NIGHT?' RICHARD asked in a tone which told her that he really didn't want to know. 'You could have called. I waited up for ages. I was worried.'

'You needn't have worried,' Amelia breezed. 'I stayed with a friend.'

'I had to feed your cat,' Richard said accusingly. 'Thanks.'

As if on cue, Eliza appeared and wound herself around Amelia's silk-stockinged legs. Richard noticed the ladder which ran upwards from her left heel.

'What friend?' he asked. As soon as the words escaped his lips he wished he could have bitten them back.

'Someone in the industry. No one you know.'

'I am in the industry, remember?'

'Oh, yeah.' Amelia laughed. 'The singing accountant. I forgot.' Richard clenched his teeth.

'Who did you stay with? I'm interested.'

'Jamie Nettles, if you must know.'

Jamie Nettles. Richard paled at the name of that posturing idiot.

'Known him long?'

'Ages,' Amelia lied. 'I'm going to have a bath. Is there any hot water?'

As Amelia jogged up the stairs, Richard finally remembered to ask, 'How was the gig?' She gave him the thumbs up sign and disappeared behind the bathroom door.

Jamie bloody Nettles. Richard knew exactly what he'd like to do to that guy with a dock leaf. They had met at the record company's Christmas party, the only time of the year when creatives, like Jamie, mixed with the proles, like Richard, who actually kept the company going when A & R's 'next-big-things' went belly-up. He wore leather trousers and high-lighted his hair. There was nothing else Richard really needed to know. Their acquaintance would have been restricted to a hair-flick and a sneer had Richard not been standing next to the prettiest girl in Finance when Jamie walked into the room.

Jamie had sashayed by, pinched the girl's bum and Richard had landed the reciprocal slap round the face. Jamie saw Richard take the flak, bought him a drink for being such a good sport and, two weeks of being best buddies later, walked off with Richard's girlfriend of the time. That dalliance hadn't lasted long of course, but Richard could never feel quite the same about his one-time dream girl again. He wondered how well Amelia had known Jamie Nettles 'for ages'.

'I forgot,' said Richard when Amelia emerged towel-wrapped from the bathroom like Botticelli's Venus from the waves. 'Jerry's secretary came round to the house this morning – in the Shogun.' Amelia's eyes narrowed. 'She dropped off some post for you.'

'Where is it?'

'Over there.' He motioned towards the mantelpiece.

Amelia sorted through the not inconsiderable pile of envelopes until she came to one with an American stamp and very familiar handwriting. Amelia turned the blue envelope over in her hands a couple of times before she took a deep breath and opened it.

'It's from my mother,' she told Richard. 'She never writes unless something has gone desperately wrong or she's about to get married.' Amelia skip-read the letter. 'And this time she's about to get married.'

Her lips pressed together in a tight smile. 'The wedding takes place next Saturday. In Las Vegas of all places. To a guy called Doug Hertzberg. He's a dentist. And his clients include Tom Cruise.' She was reading out the letter in a strong West Coast accent. 'And Mom wants me to be there – as her matron of honour. Matron. I ask you . . . She says she has already booked the tickets in my name, so I guess I'm gonna be there.'

Amelia threw the letter down onto the coffee table.

'Damn it. That means I'll have to cancel my next gig.'

'But it is your mother's wedding . . .' Richard reminded her.

'You don't understand, Richard,' Amelia said with a world-weary sigh. 'It's my mother's fifth wedding. She does this every other year.'

Chapter Five

AMELIA WAS VERY glad of her dual nationality when the Virgin flight from London touched down in Los Angeles and she was able to walk straight past the queue of true Brits waiting at immigration. She hauled her cases onto a trolley, wondering briefly how a couple of pairs of shorts and a swimsuit could possibly weigh so much, and made her way to the arrivals lounge. Her mother had told her that she had just had her hair coloured mahogany, so she looked out for a head of that shade but could see none. She was just about to get to a phone and find out why no one was there to meet her when she caught sight of a very familiar head indeed. Not mahogany, but blond. Not her mother, but Amelia's ex-lover – mark one.

'Mimi!' he jumped up and down excitedly, waving a piece of card with her name scrawled across the front of it, as if she wouldn't have recognised him. 'Mimi, it's me, Marty, over here!'

Amelia hated being called Mimi. Well, she had hated that particular abbreviation of her name ever since she and Marty had split up. He pushed forward through the crowd of people waiting to pick up loved ones and planted a hot kiss on her irritated cheek.

'Let me take that.' He wrested the luggage trolley from her grip and began to push it towards the car-park. Amelia was suddenly hit by the heat as they briefly walked through the sun. 'Why didn't you let me know you were coming? Your mother just called me. She couldn't make it to the airport because she has a tennis match at two with Mrs Hobbs that she just clean forgot. And then a residents' meeting in Bel Air. She says she will see you at the house later this evening. I said I'd pick you up . . .'

'Oh, mother,' thought Amelia. She was still trying to patch up the long-dead relationship between her daughter and one of the most eligible bachelors on this side of the Atlantic.

Marty was like a dog with two tails. He slung Amelia's luggage into the back of his red BMW six series as though it was made of polystyrene and feathers, then picked her up just as easily and twirled her around.

'I am so glad to see you, Mimi.'

'Amelia.'

'Don't be so English.'

'I am, Marty, I am . . .' She sighed. 'Hey, Dumbo, just who is my mother marrying this

56

time anyway?'

'Oh, Doug. He's a cool guy. He did these.' Marty bared his teeth for her to check out the dentistry. 'I dinged them on a rock when I was surfing off Huntingdon last month. Lost half of this one here . . . and this one was completely smashed.' He indicated a perfect denture.

'Oh, well,' Amelia sighed, 'at least I know my mother's molars are in good hands.'

Amelia went to get into the car and found herself unconsciously going for the driver's seat.

'Wrong side,' laughed Marty, using the opportunity to squeeze close by her to get to the wheel. He reached across the seats and flicked the passenger door open. She slipped in beside him, careful not to flash too much leg. Marty put the key in the ignition but didn't start the car.

'You're looking great, Mimi,' he told her as he looked deep into her eyes.

'Thanks.' She didn't like to return the compliment, though it was exactly what she was thinking. His blond hair was a little shorter than she remembered, with his heavy fringe swept back from his face. It was bleached bright blond by the sun and salt water. He smiled broadly, flashing his new white teeth, like jewels against his biscuity tan. He was wearing a light blue vest and brightly coloured board shorts that showed her that his body had lost none of its tone. As he lifted his arm to adjust the rear-view mirror, she caught a whiff of a familiar deodorant, mixed with familiar sweat, and was unable to prevent the rush of nostalgia which accompanied it. She closed her tired eyes and breathed in deeply and slowly.

'You look a touch on the pale side though, Englisher,' he was teasing her.

Amelia threw out an arm to hit him in the side. Just like old times.

'So, what exactly are you doing now?' Marty asked between mouthfuls of Caesar salad. Amelia looked around at the decor of the waterfront café as she considered her answer. What had she been doing? The sun bouncing on the water outside, the sound of ropes against sail-poles in the wind, the bronzed and beautiful people who passed them by . . . And to think that she had been living in dirty old Kentish Town when she could have stayed in her pretty summer villa on Balboa Island?

'I've been trying to get my act together.' The cliché had meaning for her in more ways than one. She had left LA for London because of the man sitting in front of her that very minute. When she had last eaten in that very café, where they were now having their lunch, she was twenty-one years old. He was six months older. Both fresh out of college. She had wanted marriage. He didn't, of course, and four years of reflection in British weather had made her see that it wouldn't really have been such a good idea after all. Compared to Jerry, Marty was still just a kid. 'Still writing songs?' he asked in a way which implied that he didn't really take her ambitions seriously.

'Yes,' she told him.

He looked surprised.

'I'm negotiating a deal, as a matter of fact.' It was a bit of an exaggeration but she was damned if Marty was going to make her feel small within an hour of stepping off the plane. And with a bit of luck, she would be making a deal in the not too distant future. Jamie Nettles had promised to look into it for her. 'And what about you? What are you doing with yourself these days?' She wanted to get Marty off the subject of her life before the holes started to become evident.

'Oh, this and that.'

As usual, Amelia reflected. Marty was fortunate to have a family rich enough to support him lovingly while he did just 'this and that', year in, year out. His father was a sought-after film producer, his mother, a fading Norwegian film star who had settled in Hollywood after a brief blaze of glory as a Bond girl in the sixties. With all that celluloid in his blood, Marty had harboured ambitions to direct, but unfortunately found it difficult to get up for anything in the morning other than the surf.

'This and that,' Amelia echoed.

'Brett and I are writing a screenplay based on the story of two surfers who find this really incredible break just off the coast of . . .'

Amelia wasn't tuned in to Marty's words. As he shovelled lettuce into his mouth and talked through it about his plans for the next year or so, she was taking in the familiar face. She took in his blue eyes, inherited from his beautiful Scandinavian mother, which sparkled excitedly as he talked about projected profits for his yet to be born production company. She took in the full lips she used to spend so much time kissing.

'You finished?' she asked him when the last mouthful of salad was gone. 'Let's go for a drive.'

Marty settled the bill with a flash of American Express and soon they were outside in the sun again. It had been warm in London but not nearly as warm as this. It was still well into the eighties though it was nearly dusk. Amelia surveyed the boats which lined the harbour as though the sight were completely new to her.

A lone roller-skater weaved in and out of the pedestrians towards them. He was oblivious to the rest of the world, lost in the music on his personal stereo to which he was no doubt matching his moves. The muscles in his legs, which flexed as he passed, touched something deep inside Amelia. She had a weakness for a pair of thick, firm thighs and the erotic possibilities which his brief appearance on the street awakened in her made her reach out and link her arm through Marty's as they walked by. He smiled at her sudden decision to touch him and resumed the contact by placing his hand on her knee when they got into the car.

It was cool enough to have the top down now. When he had picked her up at LAX it was better to have the top up and the air-conditioning on.

Marty flicked on the CD player and cranked it up as loud as it would go so that they would be able to hear the music above the roar of the powerful engine. As she settled into the deep and warm leather-covered seat, Amelia could already feel her inner thighs growing moist with the combination of the heat and the power of the automobile beneath her.

There was no doubt about it. A fast car was a great substitute for a small dick, but when the fast car was driven by someone who was not only well-off, but also well-endowed, the combination was fatal.

Once he got behind the wheel, Marty was a different guy. The aggression in his driving made him seem older somehow, more of a man. Amelia laughed to herself for thinking that the addition of a sixteen-valve engine could make him seem so much more attractive but she didn't move his hand off her knee and was disappointed when he had to pull away from her to change gears. Why the hell didn't he still drive an automatic?

They struck out onto the freeway, heading north to Malibu beach and the Bel Air beach club that Amelia had missed so much during the grey British winters. The road, busy with commuters, required a great deal of concentration and suddenly Amelia found that Marty just wasn't paying her enough attention. The engine growled beneath her, the rock music on the stereo was full of bass, making her heart beat faster, her breath come more quickly.

Now the sun was sinking and the sky turning from grey-blue to pink – a fantastic sunset being the one good side effect of the terrible smog. Amelia loved the pastel Pacific colours of Los Angeles. So different from the moody green and grey of the Atlantic beaches in Cornwall and Devon that she had visited a summer ago with Jerry. She reclined her seat a little more and looked up at the sky as they drove. From time to time a palm tree would lean over the road and cut across her view. Even the traffic lights which dangled from wires seemed exciting to her that day, especially when they were stuck on red and gave Marty the chance to turn his attention briefly back into the car.

Suddenly they hit a stretch of fairly clear road and Marty made straight for the car pool lane, making the most of having a passenger as an excuse to speed past the Porsche owners who languished one to a car in the selfish driver's queue. Amelia was lying right back, her seat fully reclined, her hair waving in the wind like a scarf, her feet braced against the floor of the car, her hand creeping down to the edge of her flirty flowery skirt.

Amelia pulled her skirt up and her pants down.

'Fuck, Amelia,' Marty gasped, as he caught sight of the action from the corner of his eye. 'I gotta concentrate on my driving.'

'I'm not asking you to join in, Marty. Just drive. Fast.'

Marty's foot went down and the sound of the

engine took on a different tone. They had to be doing a hundred now. The trees and traffic signs passing overhead became one long blue of green. Amelia opened her mouth to scream 'Yes!' but her exaltation was lost in the roar of the wind.

Her fingers, which had been twisting and tangling in her soft pubic hair, moved lower to find her fast-moistening sex. She found no resistance there, two fingers sliding straight in and out with alarming quickness. While her right hand penetrated her velvety entrance, her left hand toyed tantalisingly with her hardening clit, heightening the sensation and sending darts of excitement down her inner thighs. Using juices from her vagina, she gently lubricated the tiny clitoral nub so that she could vibrate it faster still. Her lower body was all a-tremble. Though she felt that she hardly needed to use her hands at all, lying back as she was in Marty's huge vibrator of a car.

Her mouth quivered, her face smiling and then looking as if about to cry by turns. Her breath was short, arrested, each sigh whipped away to the car travelling behind. Languidly, she turned her head to her left to look at the man beside her. Marty's hands gripped the wheel tightly, his forearms tensed. Amelia's eyes travelled down his body to his loose board shorts. An unmistakable bulge had lifted them away from his body at the crotch.

'Wanna park, Marty?' Amelia asked wickedly as she lazily continued to bring herself off.

Marty grunted a reply and turned off the freeway at the first possible opportunity, swinging the screeching car around as if it had hit a patch of black ice. Down a quiet road leading up into a junk-filled canyon, he pulled the car over onto a grassy verge that was edged by trees. Grabbing her by the hand he lifted Amelia out of the car and dragged her stumbling behind one of the parched pines, ignoring her protests that her legs were being scratched by the long, dry grass. With one hand he lifted up her skirt and, with the other, he pulled his dick out through the front of his shorts. The circumcised tip of his shaft was already glistening wetly with pre-come. Amelia divested herself of her flimsy knickers altogether and got into position.

There was no time for any more preliminaries.

'Ready?' he asked.

Marty hoisted Amelia up so that her legs were wrapped around his waist. He supported her with his strong arms while she shifted until his hard shaft hovered at the door to her desire.

'Yes. Now.'

Amelia used her thighs to pull herself in towards Marty's body and impale herself on his penis. They sighed simultaneously with the pleasure of the connection and for a moment everything seemed to be in slow motion while they enjoyed the melting sensation of coming together. Then, as though neither of them had seen a body of the opposite sex in the four years they had been apart, they began to move again.

Frantically. Sometimes in time, sometimes out of it. The powerful crashing of an ill-timed move only adding to the experience.

Amelia clung on tightly to Marty's neck, after a while letting him control the pace, pushing her and pulling her backwards and forwards. Marty had the biggest dick she had ever encountered. It stretched and filled her more deliciously than anything she had found before or since . . . And it was harder than marble now.

Marty grunted into her red hair with the exertion of holding her in position and the thunderous excitement which was building in his loins. Amelia leaned back all of a sudden and nearly pulled them both over by upsetting the balance. Marty shuffled about, with her legs still clamped around him, until he had backed her up against a tree. The dry bark scraped against her back as they moved, but she could hardly feel the pain . . . and right now she didn't really care.

Her pussy was aching for more and more and more. She knew that she was just about to come and by the frantic grunting in her hair, she could tell that Marty would not be far behind. She clutched at his shoulders, both to stop herself from falling to the ground and to have him as deep inside her as she possibly could. His fingers clenched her buttocks as he brought them into the home straight, crashing her body against his.

Marty's movements were going to pieces now as he reached explosion point. He flung his head back. His eyes were tightly closed as if his whole

65

body was trying to squeeze the orgasm out. Amelia felt his buttocks clenching beneath her calves which were still crossed tightly around the back of his body. Suddenly, he stopped his thrusting and drew her to him one final time, holding her in place as she began to feel his dick stiffening to shoot. His semen seared its way inside her.

Amelia screamed with joy as her orgasm followed quickly after. Her pussy was drenched both with his come and her own, which was forcing its way out to soak her thighs and the front of his shorts.

They collapsed onto the grass, panting with exertion. Amelia gazed up at the reddening California sky and let out a joyful laugh as Marty leant up on his elbow, kissed her nose and told her 'Welcome home'.

An hour later, Marty turned his BMW into the driveway of Amelia's mother's house in Bel Air. He turned the engine off and waited expectantly to be invited inside. Instead, Amelia opened the car door for herself, fetched her own luggage from the trunk and carried it to the porch. The key she had carried in her purse for four years still fitted the hefty lock. She opened the door and walked inside.

Marty still sat in his car. Amelia poked her head out and waved him goodbye.

'Thanks for the lift, Marty,' she called to him. 'See you in another four years or so!'

The attraction was still there, she figured, but she'd had an itch and she'd scratched it. There was no need to rub herself all over with sandpaper. As Marty gave a shrug of his handsome brown shoulders and reversed his BMW out of the drive, Amelia knew that the best thing she could do now was stay out of his way. After Jerry, she had no intention of letting herself fall in love again, particularly on the rebound with the devil she already knew too well.

Marty waved. He'd be on the beach and she'd be out of his mind by the time the sun came up the next day. As she watched the back-lights of the BMW disappear around the corner, Amelia felt just the faintest cry of disappointment from between her sticky thighs.

Chapter Six

'DARLING, DARLING, DARLING!!!'

Amelia's mother Theresa wafted into the antiqued oak kitchen in a cloud of *Giorgio*. She looked slimmer and happier than she had when Amelia last saw her on a fleeting visit to the British Isles, as Theresa was wont to call them. Behind her hovered a tall thin man with very little hair on top of his walnut-tanned head but a set of teeth that the Cheshire Cat would have killed for. Amelia guessed that this must be Doug. He introduced himself as such and kissed her on both cheeks. She couldn't help but notice that he shared her mother's taste in overpowering perfume.

'I knew you'd come, Honey Bun. Hope you didn't have to cancel anything important for your poor old mom ... I have the dress, it's in my dressing room – out of Dougie's way.' She giggled like a young virgin on her first marriage rather than a sexagenarian on her fifth. 'I was gonna get green for you because that goes best with your hair but the girl at the store said green's unlucky for weddings so I got you an Edwardian style robe with a burnt clementine velvet bodice and sleeves and ivory satin skirt instead . . .'

Doug had already wandered out into the carefully kept garden with its orange and lemon trees and was lighting up a pipe. Amelia deserted her bags on the spotless kitchen floor and followed her excited mother up the stairs to the room which had once been her own.

They flew to Vegas on the Saturday morning. Amelia's mother had tried to persuade her to have Marty there as her escort but Amelia was having none of it. True, he was a lovely guy, from a respected family, with a mansion in Stone Canyon that had an Olympic-sized pool, not to mention two ski chalets in Europe and a condo down town, but he was also the lovely guy who had once broken her heart. When the wedding was over, Amelia told Theresa, she would check out the MGM casino with the other witness, Doug's daughter Leah.

Leah was in her mid-thirties, tall like her father. She was married to an evangelist from Idaho who could not bring himself to smile on the remarriage of his father-in-law in such a city of sin. Hopefully, Amelia thought, Leah would retire at ten to say her prayers and she would be left in peace to enjoy Vegas as she really wanted to. At a blackjack table, on her own.

The drive-in wedding ceremony was suitably speedy. It was followed by a sumptuous meal in the pyramid-shaped Luxor casino-hotel. (Theresa's spiritual regressionist had told her that she was an Egyptian in a past life but Doug was unable to get the time off work to enable them to honeymoon in Cairo.) Throughout the meal, Doug and Theresa swapped glances and caresses that told Amelia they would be only too glad to see their witnesses buzz off. Amelia half-heartedly caught the bouquet her mother tossed to her as she disappeared with her new hubby into the elevator. Leah smiled approvingly and asked who was going to be the lucky man. Amelia wiped the smile off her face by saying that she was considering Mormonism since there were just too many to choose from at the present time.

The burnt clementine and ivory bridesmaid's dress soon found its way onto the bathroom floor in Amelia's slanting, windowed suite and was replaced by something a little more 'Vegas'. Leah, predictably, had wimped out of an evening at the tables. She was going to fly back to Idaho at the first possible opportunity and Amelia was free. She clipped on a pair of emerald earrings that Jerry had given her for her twenty-fourth birthday and pulled a soft green sweater embroidered with a butterfly in sparkly thread and sequins over her head. Her mother, who had bought the sweater, was right, the colour suited her daughter's hair and it didn't matter much about luck any more.

Amelia walked from the Luxor to the MGM which was just opposite, across the busy highway into a town that always moved at a snail's pace because people kept leaning out of windows to take photos and say 'oooh and aaah'. Stepping out into the gaudily lit street gave Amelia a head-rush like no other. Her pulse was raised immediately by the sights, the smells and the unnatural noise. She nodded happily at the huge billboards that flashed out alternately '$100,000 JACKPOT' and 'ALL YOU CAN EAT FOR 50 CENTS'. She looked down the road that led out of the town to the silent mountains surrounding this monument to Mammon. Then up at the indescribably gigantic lion that was the MGM hotel. She felt dwarfed, she felt exhilarated. She felt like she needed to have an orgasm.

Nearly crashing into a couple of real live cowboys with hats and rhinestones as she did so, she crossed the road and dashed inside the lion's den. A bundle of dollars which her new father-in-law had thrust into her hand after the wedding reception was burning a hole in her pocket. As the casino opened out before her, she didn't know where to start. Elegant croupiers with perfectly manicured hands dealt cards with the bored look of Oxford Street shop assistants. Theme-dressed waitresses weaved between them carrying free drinks for the punters. Young men and old ladies poured dollars into the slots of one-armed bandits as insistent as open-mouthed baby birds. To her right, a machine spilled silver dollar tokens out onto the floor. The player grovelled to scoop them up in his plastic cup while a loud electronic fanfare drew the rest of the casino's attention to the latest favourite of Lady Luck.

Amelia crossed the floor purposefully and slid silently onto an empty velvet stool at the edge of a blackjack game. She exchanged fifty dollars into tokens. The croupier dealt her in quickly and the game continued, so fast that there seemed to be nothing game-like about the whole business at all. The croupier went bust. Amelia gathered her winnings and prepared for the next game, doubling her stake. If you're going to gamble, Jerry used to say, you might as well gamble big. Well, ten dollars wasn't quite big, but by the end of the evening she would get there.

A waitress came and took her order, returning minutes later with a double dark rum and Coke over ice. And another. And another. Amelia sat at the same table until she had increased her pile of tokens to seventy-five and doubted that she would actually be able to stand straight if she did get up.

'Quit while you're ahead, eh?'

Amelia swivelled around on her stool, her hands full of bright plastic tokens, to come face to face with the last person she had expected, or wanted, to see in Vegas that night. His bow tie hanging undone around his neck, his waistcoat open – a sign that he had just had a pretty good meal – Jerry Anson stood behind her with a cigar burning in the corner of his mouth.

'Jerry? What are you doing here?'

'I could ask the same of you.'

'It's a small world.' Amelia's automatic reaction to the sight of Jerry's face, a smile, had been swiftly replaced by a less friendly façade.

'No,' said Jerry, about to use one of his favourite corrections, 'it's a big world and there are a lot of coincidences.'

Amelia stood up to go but Jerry settled himself on her stool, pulling her down onto his knee before she could protest. 'You can be my mascot, Amy,' he told her. He put his hand in his pocket and pulled out a crumpled fistful of hundred-dollar bills. The croupier changed a thousand dollars into gambling chips. Jerry put the whole thousand on the table and won first time.

'You are my lucky star,' he sang to the squirming girl on his knee.

'Let go of me, Jerry,' Amelia snarled. 'Your "Personal Assistant" might get jealous.'

'She isn't here.' Jerry's speech was slurred – the result of too many hospitality whiskies. 'She's looking after the office. And anyway, I wasn't sleeping with her. I was sleeping with Mac's girl . . .'

Before he could tell her that it was all over now, Amelia landed a stinging slap right on Jerry's jaw. He tumbled backwards, tipping her onto the floor as he fell. He hit his head on the edge of another table and lay, out cold, on the plush red carpet. The croupier had stopped the game. The punters gathered round him in a collective gasp.

'You all right?' asked a Texan gentleman who helped Amelia to her feet. 'Was he bothering you?'

'He's been bothering me for four years!!' Amelia shouted indignantly as she stood over Jerry's prone body, her hands on her hips. 'You low-down sonofabitch, why don't you just stay out of my life!'

Jerry clutched his head and groaned.

'Get up, you creep,' Amelia snarled, 'so I can knock you down again!'

The crowd was growing. This was better than a free trip to Universal Studios.

Jerry pulled himself giddily to his feet with the aid of a little blue-haired lady who didn't like the look of the harridan with the funny accent haranguing the poor English gent. He tried to look at Amelia, but his eyes wouldn't focus. Blood was beginning to seep from a cut on the top of his head.

'Oh mi gad!' the blue-haired lady shrieked. 'The man is bleeding. Will somebody purleese call a paramedic.' Mobile phones were pressed into action all around and within seconds a first-aider was at Jerry's side. Amelia was quickly forgotten as the crowd surged around her to be nearer to Jerry and hear the verdict. Someone got out a video camera and started to film the whole debacle but was quickly shooed away by the staff.

'Concussion,' someone said gravely. 'What's his name? Who's he with?'

Amelia was pushed to the front, protesting as she went. 'I am most certainly not with him—' but the first-aider only took in her vaguely similar accent and the brief look of recognition in Jerry's swimming eyes.

'She's his girlfriend,' said someone, who hadn't seen the punch, helpfully.

'Is he gonna sue the casino for having sharp tables?' said someone else, worriedly.

'I saw everything. I'll be a witness,' said the granny with the blue hair.

'I'm okay, I'm okay.' Jerry was shooing the spectators away with floppy hands. 'It's just a little cut. I just need to have a little lie-down.'

'Do you have a hotel room?'

'He's staying in mine,' said the blue-haired lady.

'Is that right?' the first-aider asked the inert body on the floor.

'No, it is not right,' Amelia outglared the blue-haired lady. 'He doesn't even know her. He's staying with me. I'm in the Luxor. Can somebody help me get him across the road?'

Two Texans obliged and soon a dazed Jerry was bandaged up and undercover in bed. Amelia's bed. She had to keep him awake, they said. To make sure that he didn't go into a coma. Jerry thanked them gratefully and waved regally as they left. Amelia sat on the edge of her lovely double bed, which was now full of her nightmare bedmate, and scowled.

'Do these beds vibrate?' Jerry asked. 'I stayed in

75

a motel here once where the beds vibrated.' He looked around for a slot to stick a dollar in.

'Don't make such ridiculous small-talk with me, Jerry. I'm already regretting rescuing you from that blue-haired witch. All I want to know is, what are you doing here?'

'You offered to let me stay in your room.'

'No, smart-arse, I mean what are you doing here in Vegas?'

Jerry took a theatrically painful drink out of the glass of icy water that stood beside the bed. 'I'm only in Vegas for the weekend. I got called in to sort out some fiasco of a second album The Dolphins were recording in LA. Their producer stropped off when he got rebuffed by the drummer, or something like that. Love, eh?' he added with a laugh. 'I've got a couple of days spare while they sleep off a big record company binge. Vegas is just recreation. I came out here to meet Michael.' The mention of Jerry's least desirable friend made Amelia snort with derision. 'But that's enough about me. What about you?'

'My mother got married today.'

'What? Again?'

'Yes. Again.'

'Anyone nice?'

'His name is Doug Hertzberg and he's a dentist to the stars, no less.'

Jerry spat a mouthful of water out with a laugh.

'It's not that funny.' Amelia flopped backwards onto the bed so that she and Jerry were now lying side by side. Him under the sheets. Her on top.

His hand tentatively sought hers. She brushed it away.

'I've missed you,' she thought she heard him say, as she started to drift into a woozy, alcohol-induced doze.

'Oh yeah.'

The combination of jet-lag and the excitement of her mother's fifth wedding were too much for Amelia and she soon forgot to check that Jerry wasn't slipping into a coma and fell asleep herself. When she awoke the next morning, he wasn't beside her. She wondered for a moment whether it had all been a dream. Then the sound of a running shower told her that it had not. She rolled over and buried her face in a pillow which reeked of Jerry's aftershave. Oh no, oh no, she thought. What had she done? She felt a little better when she noticed that at least she was still fully clothed.

Jerry emerged from the steamy bathroom, rubbing what was left of his hair dry with a fluffy towel. He tenderly touched the little bump which had formed at the back of his head and winced. He was still standing though and if he was perfectly honest with himself, a hangover probably counted for ninety per cent of the headache he was feeling right now.

He started to dress, chastely, beneath his towel. Amelia watched him, eyes narrowed, suspicious.

'I'll just get dressed and then I'll be out of your way.' His face had the look of a puppy that had just made a mess and was anticipating a kick. 'I'll check into a motel down the road and spend the rest of the day getting some more sleep. God knows I need it. Thanks for looking after me, Amelia . . . for making sure that I didn't slip into a coma . . .'

It was working. Amelia lay on her back with her hand over her eyes and sighed.

'Okay, okay. I've got this room for another night. You can sleep off your accident here.'

'Oh, thank you, darling.' He bounded over to the bed and planted a kiss on her forehead.

'But just don't touch me, OK?'

'What?' he asked. 'Not even a little bit?'

He grabbed her around the waist and dug his fingers between her ribs. The effect of his tickling was like an electric shock. Her body tensed and flipped about like a fish out of water. Jerry kept it up until she was writhing, helpless and breathless, all over the bed, knocking the pillows to the floor and grabbing at the sheets in a vain attempt to protect herself.

'Stop it, stop it,' she giggled ineffectually.

'Only if you'll kiss me,' Jerry said slyly.

'I'll . . . do . . . anything!' Amelia gasped in desperation.

Suddenly, Jerry ceased his torture and pulled her close. His face was serious, as was hers. Closing his eyes, he moved in for the promised kiss. Amelia kept her eyes open until he had come too close.

'Amelia,' he murmured, gathering her tickle-loosened body up in his arms. Momentarily forgetting they had ever been apart, she let her arms wrap languidly around his neck as their lips met and moved together, bringing back all the magic and erasing the pain which had forced her from his touch. Soon her hands were caressing him, twisting the slightly too long hair at the back of his head. Smoothing across his naked shoulders until she found her favourite little mole. His hands echoed hers through the barrier of her soft green sweater, until he felt he had probably regained licence to pull it out of the way.

'Amelia,' he whispered again.

They broke away from each other for just a second while Amelia lifted her arms to help him pull the sweater off. She was wearing a silky camisole beneath to stop the wool from making her itch. Jerry let his hands slide backwards and forwards on the silk for a while before that too found its way to the floor. He studied her face and smiled when he noticed that she was wearing the earrings he had given her and that the amber pendant which had been his last present to her still hung around her neck.

'I really have missed you,' he murmured.

'Yeah,' she said again, but this time there was a happy laugh in her voice.

Jerry dipped his head to the familiar breasts and carefully kissed them on each nipple as though he was greeting long lost friends. Then he returned to the first one, sucking the nipple into his mouth until it stood erect like a tiny ruby

79

crown on a splendid dome. He did the same to the other, working it upright with his agile tongue. Amelia gazed at the top of his head for a while as he licked and kissed her, then closed her eyes, blocking out all sensation except touch. Jerry reached up and took her hands by the wrists and held them above her head while he let his lips wander across the sensitive join of breast and armpit. Amelia shivered at the faintly tickly feeling it gave her. Jerry's firm grip on her wrists prevented her from moving herself out of his way.

When he had kissed her from the base of her long throat to her waist, Jerry let go of Amelia's hands. She reached for him straight away, running her fingers lazily down his chest, through the greying hair on the tanned skin. Propped up on one elbow beside her, Jerry smiled contentedly as Amelia found the place where he had tucked the end of the towel in to secure it around his waist. She pulled it free.

'I've missed you too, Jerry.' It was her turn to say that now as her fingers lovingly caressed the familiar penis that had been hiding beneath the towel. The stiffening shaft pulsed ever so slightly as if in accord. Jerry traced the line of Amelia's body down to her navel and kissed her lightly on the nose. Then he gently removed her hand from his balls and rolled her over so that she lay on her back.

Jerry began to fumble with the belt at Amelia's waist. Impatiently she reached down to give him a hand, wriggling her hips free of the denim. Jerry clambered between her parted legs and pushed them upwards by the ankles so that her knees were bent towards the ceiling. Then he slid back down the silky sheets so that his chin rested for a moment on her belly. Amelia hoped she knew what was coming and shivered in anticipation.

She closed her eyes as she first felt Jerry's fingers find the delicate folds of her labia. Carefully, so carefully, he was parting them to reveal the succulent pink surface inside, which was already slick and shiny like the inside of a shell. For a short while, Jerry just gazed at the promise which lay before him, while Amelia breathed heavily but measuredly. Then it was time for Jerry to dip his head, to seek out her deepest secrets with his tongue.

As his tongue touched her clitoris, Amelia's legs bucked and twisted to one side. Waves of sensation rushed through her body to converge at that most sensitive spot. Jerry took her hips firmly in his hands and held her still, his tongue tantalising her like a live wire applied directly to her clitoris. Expertly, he flicked his agile tongue around and around, doing to her clitoris what he had latterly done to her nipples. Spurred on by the soft sounds of pleasure which floated down towards him from the pillows, Jerry increased his pace. Amelia's hands suddenly clutched at his head. She didn't know whether to hold him still, try to stop him from driving her over the edge, or to push his tongue down and further inside her.

Jerry pushed his tongue inside her. Gently probing at first, like a hummingbird in search of nectar. Flickering around the entrance to her vagina. Then going more deeply, until he was using his tongue like a penis to thrust into her, driving her so crazy with desire for him that she could barely lie still. When Jerry climbed back up the bed to kiss her, his chin was wet. He was smiling ecstatically.

'Can't think of anything I'd like better for breakfast . . .' he murmured.

She swatted him with a pillow.

'Come here,' she said, using his erect penis as a stick to pull him closer to her. Jerry moved towards her quickly, mindful of the potential for pain in the situation. Amelia wrapped one arm around his neck as she kissed him. Her other hand was busy down below, slicking the foreskin on his stiff shaft backwards and forwards until she was satisfied with the hardness in her hand.

'Will you make love to me, Jerry?' she asked him breathlessly. He didn't need to be asked again. He tipped Amelia carefully back onto the bed as though she were made of alabaster and positioned himself between her thighs. Her hand was still between them, helping Jerry to find her pulsing vagina the first time. As he penetrated her, he kept his eyes fixed on hers. They were swimming with tears which were strangely at odds with the smile on her lips. He moved slowly, as he had done the last time they made love, just hours before she left him alone in his flat. It was as if he was trying to make better the damage he had done to their relationship by using his body as a tool of worship. Amelia pulled his face down to hers and kissed him deeply as they moved together.

This was what they meant by 'making love'. This was sex that could heal, she thought. Sex that bonds.

Though they were taking things slowly, she could sense that Jerry was almost there. His face had taken on that peculiar look of mingled pain and pleasure. He was holding his breath, then letting it out in great, noisy gasps. Amelia clasped him tightly between her thighs and closed him inside her arms. Inside her, his penis twitched and danced, sending jets of semen deep into her. Her own body pulsed faster and faster at its depths, echoing each of Jerry's climactic thrusts. When they had both finished coming, she wrapped her legs around him so that he couldn't pull out. She wanted him there forever – again.

Jerry pushed the aerial of his mobile phone back down.

'I have to go, sweetheart. The bassist has finally woken up and we're going back into the studio this afternoon. Finishing off, I hope. I'll see you when I get back to London, yes? In about a week, maybe two.'

'You will call me, won't you?'

'Of course, sweetheart, of course.' Jerry kissed Amelia on the forehead, slipped the phone into his pocket and was gone.

Amelia had a brief rendezvous with her mother and stepfather in a restaurant at Caesar's Palace before they drove off to honeymoon for a couple of days in Palm Springs. When she had bid them goodbye, promising to be back in the States before her mother next changed her hair colour, she called the airport and changed her ticket so that she could fly straight to London from Vegas instead of bothering to go back via Los Angeles. She didn't really have anyone she needed to see there now. Jerry would be working in the studio and she knew of old that he wouldn't want to be distracted. Since she had been educated in England, she had no old school pals there and as for Marty, well, as she'd said when he dropped her off, she'd see him again in four years. No, she would go straight back to London and get on with her life. If she was going to get things together with Jerry again she would have to make sure that things were different this time. She would have her own career so that she didn't spend all her days moping about the house while he was working, and smothering him while he was at home.

She would make Jerry proud of her.

Chapter Seven

AMELIA WASN'T ABLE to get a plane home that night after all. The travel agent had managed to doublebook her seat and so she found herself stuck in Vegas until the next afternoon. She rang Jerry at the studio. He couldn't come to the phone. She managed to stop herself from dialling the final digit of Marty's number, just, even though she knew that he would drive out to meet her in a flash. She was just flicking through the channels on her three-million-channel cable television when the phone by the bedside actually rang for her.

Amelia snatched the receiver up.

'Hello?'

'Miss ... We have somebody for you in reception.'

'Really? Who is it?'

'It's a Ms Lusardi.'

'Lusardi?' Amelia heard the receptionist cover

the mouthpiece and ask her guest for her first name.

'Ms Karis Lusardi.'

'Karis?' Amelia shrieked. A broad smile of recognition spread across her lips. 'Karis Lusardi! I don't believe it. Send her on up.'

It seemed just seconds later that Karis Lusardi stood at the door of Amelia's hotel room with her Louis Vuitton overnight bag in one hand and a bottle of Bollinger in the other. Still reeling from the surprise of her old friend's sudden arrival, Amelia stood aside to let her in. Karis dumped the bag on the bed and handed Amelia the bottle. Then she hugged her so tightly, Amelia thought her ribs were caving in.

'Dump that in the chiller, thriller,' said Karis in her familiar rhyme. Amelia moved towards the mini-bar but was going too slowly for her impatient friend, who whisked past her, grabbed the bottle back and did the job herself, fishing out a miniature gin and tonic as she did so.

'Aaaah, that's better. Shame they make them so small,' she sighed as she knocked it back straight. Amelia winced. 'So, Miss English,' Karis began, 'just what do you think you're doing? Coming back to the City of Angels and not letting your very best friend and social adviser know that you're in town? I only found out you were over here because I bumped into that dork Marty at Salty Dog's. Marty Dorkface! I just can't believe you saw Marty Dorkface and you didn't come and see me. I don't know why I bothered to seek you out at all, you fair-weather friend. But for now I guess you are forgiven. Come here.'

Karis flopped onto the bed, her jet-black hair spreading out around her like a fan. She was wearing red, as usual. A tight button-through top that was only fastened as high as her black Wonderbra. Her legs were covered, in places, by a pair of ripped black jeans. She kicked off her shiny red high heels and made herself more comfortable. Amelia sat down beside her to offer an explanation.

'When I asked Mom if you were about, she said you had gone away to Alaska with some horny fisherman you met in Palm Springs . . .'

'What?' Karis looked momentarily confused. 'Fisherman? What fisherman?' She furrowed her brow while she mentally flicked through a card index of the last four years' hot dates. 'Oh, hang on, yes. I remember. His name was Andy. He had a cute body, great butt. To die for, in fact. But he wasn't a fisherman, Amelia. He owned a fishing fleet, for heaven's sake. Do you think I would go to Alaska to spend my life with some guy who comes home with his hands all covered in squid ink?' She rolled her eyes in mock despair.

'So what happened to him?' Amelia asked, more out of politeness than interest.

'I moved back down here with a writer I met in Anchorage.'

'Karis!' Like Marty, Amelia's best friend hadn't changed a bit.

'But that's all over now. He was into all sorts of

weird shit. Animals and stuff.'

'Don't tell me about it,' Amelia winced. 'But I imagine there must be someone new by now.'

'Well . . .' Karis's face took on the expression which signalled a new conquest and a big story. 'As a matter of amazing fact, I think I just may have met the love of my life.'

'The love of your life?'

'Yeah.' Her face took on a look of intense excitement. She sat up on the bed while she was speaking. 'It's early days.'

'How early?'

'Three days. Maybe four. What day is it today?' Karis counted the days back on her fingers. Amelia just rolled her eyes. 'But you know how it is when you just, you know, just know?'

Amelia guessed that a nod was probably the appropriate response at this juncture.

'I met him at The Batcave in Santa Monica. You won't have been there. It's new. Opened last October. Batman theme.'

'Funnily enough.'

'Anyway, I saw him across the top of my date's shoulder and it was like, wow. Drums crashed. Lightning flashed. There he is . . . There is the man for me. For ever.' She crossed her heart to illustrate the fact. 'So, while Butch was in the men's room I made maximum eye contact with this wonderful guy, which was reciprocated, of course, and I scribbled a little note on a page from my organiser which I slipped to Mr Gorgeous as I went to powder my nose.'

'Who's Butch?'

'Oh, some football player I met on the beach. Nice enough. You know the type. Big but thick . . .'

'And did Butch see you making a play for this other guy?'

'No, no, no! I was *très* discreet. Anyway, the note said, "meet you in the hallway in ten seconds". He followed me out there and we kissed.' Karis put her hand to her heart. 'Amelia, it was the most incredible kiss I have ever shared with a man.'

'You just kissed?' Amelia asked. That wasn't Karis's usual style.

'Well, we had a bit of a grope, but we couldn't do much because Butch was still there. So, anyway, we swapped vitals and agreed to meet in a sweet bar by the marina on Tuesday night.'

'What were his vitals?' Amelia asked.

'A good seven by the feel of it.'

'I meant vitals like his name, Karis.'

'Oh Amelia, you know me. I was off my head. I think it began with a J. Jeffrey. Yeah, that was it. Jeffrey. He's in music. Funny accent. I'll recognise his face . . . I hope. I can't wait to see if the engine matches the exterior, if you know what I mean!'

Amelia couldn't help laughing. It was always the same with Karis. Always in love with love. The more outrageous and mysterious and downright dangerous her meetings, the better. Picking up a new date while she was already out with one guy was nothing new or unusual for this particular good-time girl. Amelia remembered fondly the time when Karis had deliberately speeded backwards and forwards past a traffic cop she fancied until he booked her and she got his number on the back of her ticket.

'Is that champagne cold yet?' Karis asked.

'It's only been in the chiller for three seconds, Karis,' Amelia reprimanded. 'Can't you wait?'

'Oh well, I like it warm.'

Amelia retrieved the bottle. Karis sat on the edge of the bed and held out two plastic cups while Amelia popped open the cork. The warm champagne bubbled furiously and a great deal of the pale golden liquid missed the cups completely and dribbled down Amelia's arm until it dripped off her elbow. Karis grabbed her former playmate by the wrist and twisted her about until Amelia's elbow was dripping straight into Karis's open, scarlet-lipped mouth. She flicked out her pink tongue to catch the shining amber teardrops.

'Cut that out,' Amelia laughed. Even her elbows could be unbearably ticklish at times. Karis let go of Amelia's elbow and returned her attention to the plastic cups which were fizzing nicely. She downed her share of the booze in one gulp. 'I don't know how you can do that,' Amelia said. 'The bubbles in this stuff get right up my nose.'

'Practice, dear Amelia, practice. I like to line my stomach with champagne. It doesn't give you a hangover.'

'Karis, I think you may be a lush.'

'No, that's not true because if I was a lush I would drink all the time. I only drink with a meal.'

'We're not eating now.'

'No, but we will be. Come on, let's go and get something inside us.' Amelia winced at the innuendo with which Karis always invested her words. Karis jumped to her feet and crammed them back inside her dangerous red shoes. Grabbing the half-empty champagne bottle from Amelia's hand, she made for the door and stood there, waiting for the bemused redhead to catch up. 'What do you fancy? Champagne and corndogs?'

'Sounds great,' said Amelia. 'You're on.'

The array of choice for eating out in Las Vegas proved just too bewildering and so they eventually found themselves plumping for an 'All you can eat for $3' buffet in Circus Circus, the legendary casino where circus acts still performed nightly in the big ring which nestled between the slot machines and the gaming tables. Nobody really seemed to pay much attention to the girls on their flying trapezes any more. For the gamblers, the slot machines held a more personal reward. And now that Circus Circus had one of the biggest water-chute rides in the world dangling between casino and car-park it would take Elvis unicyling naked to bring the appeal of the Big Top back. Amelia sat opposite Karis on a plastic chair and picked at her potato salad, while

Karis filled her in on the comings and going of those simple Los Angeles folk since Amelia had left for England.

'Virginia Schneider,' Karis said, waving her fork to catch Amelia's full attention. 'Mousy hair, big nose? Now there's one hell of an unlucky girl. You know she got engaged to Mark Warbler straight out of college. Buck teeth, BMW six series? You know the guy, you do. Well, last October he left Virginia for some Swiss girl that his married sister was employing as an au-pair, and then, to top it all, Virginia got one of those exploding breast jobs. It was nasty, by all accounts. Silicone and heli-skiing just don't mix. Boy, am I glad these are real.' Karis cupped her own breasts and bumped them up and down. Amelia cringed and hid her eyes with her hand.

'Hey!' Karis's bouncing had earned her the avid attention of an admirer on the other side of the cafeteria. Karis tossed back her raven hair. 'Amelia, would you get a load of that cowboy?'

Amelia swivelled around on her chair to see just who Karis was raving about now. The cowboy tipped his studded white hat at her and smiled a slow, broad smile. Karis coyly feigned a flush and waved her hand in front of her face to cool her cheeks down. The cowboy was already purposefully getting to his Cuban-heeled feet.

'Amelia,' sighed Karis like a Southern belle, 'I think I just met the love of my life – mark four.'

'Well, good evening to you two lovely ladies.'

Now that he was standing right in front of them, the cowboy tipped his hat again.

'Good evening to you too,' replied Karis, mimicking his Texan accent as her eyes flickered between his cute little face and his tight denim crotch.

'Mind if I pull up a chair?' he asked, already drawing one up. He turned it around and sat astride the seat, his arms lying along the top of the back rest. He pushed back the brim of his hat with two fingers, like a child's representation of a gun, and his knowing eyes drifted lazily from one girl to the other, making it obvious that it wasn't only Karis who had drawn him across from his corner chair. Amelia focused on the little silver pistol motif which formed the fastening of his bootlace tie. Oh boy, she thought. Only that morning she had decided to make a go of her relationship with Jerry again and here was grey-eyed temptation, already putting itself very much in her way.

'So where y'all from?' he asked to break the uncomfortable silence.

'Santa Monica,' replied Karis.

'And you, little blue eyes?' he said, turning his unsettling attention to Amelia again.

'London,' she stuttered.

'London, England?' he asked, looking a little amazed.

'London, England,' she confirmed.

'Well, I ain't never seen such a pretty-looking English girl before. Do you want to come and have a cup of tea with me?' he said in his best Cockney accent. He laughed at his own bad joke. Amelia knew that she shouldn't be intrigued by this chap-wearing wide boy but there was something unnerving about his smile. Something sexual. And he knew it. Karis was laughing with him, throwing her head back to expose her beautiful lithe throat to him as she did so. Twiddling her hair flirtatiously. The presence of this handsome stranger had all but obliterated the friendship between the two women.

'And what're your names?'

'I'm Karis,' the dark-haired girl answered languidly, 'and this is my very good friend Amelia.' Amelia nodded.

'Well, I'm mighty pleased to make your acquaintance, Miss Karis and Miss Amelia. My name is Ricky and this here,' he gestured to another cowboy who appeared like magic behind him, is Bud. Say hello to the ladies, Bud.'

'Hello to the ladies, Bud,' parroted the standing guy. They were a regular double act. Amelia took the newcomer in. He looked a little older than Ricky, who must have been in his late twenties. A little taller, too. Thicker-set. A wide black moustache travelled across his upper lip. Ricky was clean-shaven. As fair as Ricky was, Bud was dark – even in the clothes that they were wearing. Ricky wore pale blue jeans and a white shirt with silver details. Bud wore an identical shirt in black and gold. Amelia wondered if these guys got dressed together for effect as she and Karis had done when they were younger.

'You girls want to come and shoot some craps with us?' Bud asked.

Karis was already on her feet. 'Yeah. Why not?'

As they followed the tight denim-covered butts out onto the gaming floor, Karis and Amelia hung back a little to get the evening's tactics clear.

'Ricky's mine, I think, little sister,' Karis purred, already sure that her catch for the evening was in the bag.

'Oh what?' Amelia protested. 'That's unfair.'

'OK,' Karis conceded. 'We'll shoot it out. Whoever takes most money away from the table in a half hour gets first choice.'

Chapter Eight

KARIS AND AMELIA sat side by side at the table. Bud was to Amelia's left, Ricky to the right of Karis. The boys were placing pretty big stakes, bigger than Amelia had expected. Ricky put down fifty dollars, Bud doubled his friend's stake and put down a hundred. He eyed the girls for a reaction. Karis raised her eyebrows to Amelia. To one of her regular dates, a hundred bucks was just the tip you left the coat-check boy. The croupier rolled her dice. Bud lost. Ricky collected his winnings and was unable to suppress a smile.

Bud pulled his chair a little closer to the table and to Amelia. His leg now rested against the length of her taut thigh. He shifted position and put a hand just above her knee to steady himself. Amelia felt a warm prickle run along the back of her neck. Yeah, Ricky was definitely the pretty one of the pair, but Bud had something altogether more exciting about him. It was almost as if he emanated danger. As the croupier began another game, Amelia felt Bud's arm slide slowly around the back of her chair. He was almost touching her . . . but not quite.

This time around, Bud's luck was in. Ricky nodded in defeat and pushed his hat back again so that its brim framed his boyish face like a halo. Karis had her shiny scarlet varnished fingertips on Ricky's thigh, right up near his crotch. Amelia felt a smile creep across her lips at the sight of Ricky's tightening trousers beneath that professional hand. His face was reddening involuntarily. Karis, however, looked straight ahead at the game with the inscrutable expression of the Sphinx.

Suddenly, while the table was busy with people collecting their winnings, Bud grabbed Amelia's hand and pulled it down roughly to his own button fly. 'Feel this,' he hissed, pressing her fingers down into the denim. 'This is for you.' Amelia was crimson. The assembled punters were too busy concentrating on the game to notice, or to care.

Bud held her hand so tightly to his hard prick that she felt the bones might crack in his crushing grip. His unexpectedly rough gesture had shocked her at first but now she could feel the blush which had started in her cheeks spreading elsewhere. She moved slightly in her seat until she could feel the seam of her jeans rubbing against her labia. Bud leant closer to her and whispered hotly in her ear. The croupier smiled as though she knew exactly what he was saying.

'What do you say we leave these two here and go back to my room right this minute, Amelia?'

Amelia swallowed nervously. A small voice inside her momentarily questioned the sense in going back to this virtual stranger's room. And the morality of it in view of that morning's renewed vows. But Bud's breath in her ear was fanning the heat building inside her and she nodded.

'I'll just tell Karis where we're going,' she gulped. 'So that she can find us later on.' He wouldn't try anything too funny if he thought that someone else might come looking for her. Bud smiled like a spider that was well-prepared to bide a little more time for his chosen fly. He turned back to the table for one last game.

Karis listened to Amelia's excuses and winked. She was pleased enough that she was being left to her own devices with the blond guy for at least a short while.

'So Ricky is mine for the night, then?' Karis whispered excitedly.

'I didn't say that . . . He is for now.'

'OK. We'll join you in an hour, yeah?'

'Just an hour?'

'I don't want you to wear Bud out before I've had the chance to take a ride on that moustache!'

Amelia cringed.

'Anyway,' Karis continued, 'I thought you agreed with me that the more, the merrier.'

'You know I do. But do you think these guys will be into that? Cowboys are normally pretty straight when it comes down to it.' At that moment, Ricky looked across to see what they were talking about and held Amelia's gaze for a second with his light grey eyes.

'All guys are into it, Amelia,' said Karis, as though she was talking about peanut butter and jelly sandwiches. 'And besides, I haven't seen *you* in so long.' Karis placed heavy emphasis on the "you" and laid her spare hand on Amelia's unattended leg. Amelia blushed still deeper. Her hand tightened involuntarily at a particularly vivid memory of a long ago beach party scene. Amelia's hand was still in Bud's crotch. He relayed his pleasure by gently squeezing her fingers.

'I'll see you in an hour, then,' Amelia said breathlessly. 'Chalet C 15. It's on the other side of the car-park. Oh, and you will make sure you knock before you come in?'

Karis gave a little chuckle and turned back to the game.

Seeing that Karis and Amelia had made their plans, Bud pushed his pile of chips over to Ricky. 'Don't lose it all at once,' he quipped. Then he got to his feet and dragged Amelia away from the table in the direction of the exit.

They had to pass through a dismal multi-storeyed car-park on their way to Bud's room. They walked a little way apart – he didn't even try to hold her hand – but, as soon as they were out of the general flow of human traffic, Bud suddenly pushed Amelia up against a cold, grey wall and began to kiss her. To devour her. His tongue forced her teeth apart and flickered inside her mouth like a serpent's fork. His lips crushed hers until she was sure that they must be bruised. His moustache was rough against her soft face.

There was no time for the formalities of polite courtship with Bud. As his mouth seemed to draw the breath from her body with its force, his hands were almost immediately beneath her sweater, pushing her bra out of the way to grab at her tender breasts, squeezing them tightly with almost total disregard for the fact that she was made of flesh and blood.

After ten seconds or so, he grabbed one of her hands and pulled it down to his crotch again. As he set about kissing her neck, biting a path down to her collar-bone, Amelia felt his hard shaft twitch beneath her palm and let out a gasp of anticipation. Through his jeans it felt so long, so rigid. She hoped that she wouldn't be disappointed. Quickly she set to work on his button fly. Bud helped her by loosening his belt. He worked his dick out through the narrow gap. Soon his shaft was bobbing in front of her in the still air of the car-park, then pressing into her stomach as he once more pulled her tighter against him for a kiss.

Amelia worked one of her hands between their frantic bodies and wrapped her fingers around the penis's wide girth. She began to slick the warm foreskin slowly back and forth. Bud was undoing her jeans now. Forcing his own hand down between the tight covering of denim and her skin until he reached her mound. Excited as she was by the build-up to this moment, which they had shared at the gaming table, and by the impressive size of the organ she now held in her hand, Amelia knew that she was already wet. Bud probed roughly at the lips of her vagina with the tip of his middle finger until he found a gap between them and was able to slip suddenly inside.

Amelia gasped with pleasure. 'Let's do it now,' she breathed low in his ear. The combination of Bud's hot breath on her neck and his fingers at her clit was almost paralysing her with desire.

'We can't do it here,' he replied gruffly, his voice muffled by the flesh of her throat. 'If you had a skirt on maybe, but not with jeans. You'd have to take them down and the whole world would see your ass.'

'I don't care,' Amelia laughed, but Bud was already extricating his hand from her pants so that they could abandon their bleak location and head for his motel room.

He had taken a cheap suite in one of the low blocks to the side of the car-park. He carefully guided her inside the anonymous chalet with an incongruously chivalrous gesture. The television was running, tuned into MTV. A hard rock band were thudding out a song about the blood of virgins, with a commentary by Beavis and Butthead. Amelia barely had time to take in the room, which was so different from her luxurious pad at the Luxor, before Bud was edging her backwards, slipping her sweater over her head and off as he did so, and pushing her down onto the scratchy, musty-smelling blanket that covered the bed. Her dusty shoes dropped from her feet to the floor.

Amelia's jeans were still undone from their tangle in the car-park. Bud tore them from her roughly so that she was dressed only in her bra and panties. His eyes were looking through her, seeing nothing about her but her body. They were hungry, desperate eyes that sent a shiver of delicious fear through Amelia's vulnerable bones. Bud pulled his own tight jeans down only as far as his knees. He wore nothing beneath and Amelia's eyes were drawn instantly to his dick, standing proudly out in front of him. She longed to take it inside her mouth and draw him, oh so slowly, to the brink of pleasure. She wanted to make a real meal of him. But she knew already that that wasn't going to happen.

Bud carelessly flipped Amelia over onto her front and tore her delicate white panties off. His hands slipped quickly beneath her waist, pulling her down towards him until she was half off the bed, her feet on the floor, her bottom high in the air. She could feel his dick already nudging insistently at her upturned labia. With just two determined thrusts Bud found the licence he was looking for and was suddenly deep inside.

The strength of his thrusting nearly threw Amelia flat on her face. She braced her arms, locking her elbows to keep herself steady as he pounded into her. His balls slapped against her each time he went in to the hilt, keeping time with the bass of the song which blared from the television.

After the initial surprise of his brutal entry, Amelia found herself pushing back to meet him, excited not just by the friction between their bodies but by the anonymity of the position she now found herself in. This man with his rough hands around her smooth waist could be anyone. Anyone at all. She hardly knew his face. Amelia screwed her eyes tightly shut and tried to focus on a face in her mind. She was nowhere near achieving a picture of her fantasy man when she felt Bud's fingers tighten harder and harder on her waist. His thrustings began to fall apart, become deeper, slower. His breathing staggered. He was almost wheezing. All the time he used his hands to pull her body more and more firmly against his.

He grunted suddenly. Amelia threw her head back in a sympathetic sigh as the hot spurts of his sticky semen began to fill her. He continued to thrust until it was all gone from him and beginning to run down her inner thigh. Then, without so much as a word or whisper of endearment, he withdrew from her abruptly, used her pretty little panties to wipe his dick dry, and collapsed on the bed beside her. His chest was heaving with the exertion of his climax. Amelia surveyed him from her position of all fours. He made as if to speak but the words came out only as gasps. Finally Amelia rested on her elbows beside him.

'Is that it?' she asked humorously. 'We haven't even started yet.'

Chapter Nine

EXACTLY AN HOUR after they had left the casino, Amelia heard the tinkle of familiar champagne-fuelled laughter floating in through the window of Bud's dismal room. Bud was fast asleep. That really did seem to be that . . . for the moment at least. Amelia lay on her back beside him and looked at the fan which was spinning lazily in the corner. Bud's efforts had only just warmed her up. Thank heavens the cavalry was about to arrive.

Karis was outside the door now, whispering loudly about not wanting to disturb any funny business. Ricky was protesting that they shouldn't look in on the others. Karis was insisting that they did. She hiccupped, and then knocked briskly at the door. Amelia swung it open and Karis, who had been leaning against it and not expecting such prompt attention, nearly fell in. Ricky tumbled in with her. He had been leaning against Karis.

Karis regained her balance and surveyed the room. She pulled a disappointed face. She surveyed the bed, and Cowboy Bud, flat out upon it. She pulled another disappointed face.

'That good, huh? How was the moustache?'

'I am going to have extremely bad beard burn,' was all Amelia could be bothered to say.

'Oh well.'

'How's it going with the Milky Bar Kid?' Amelia whispered.

'Not great,' replied Karis. 'After all that bravado in the casino, I think in reality he's just a little shy.'

Karis and Amelia turned to look at Ricky. He was still standing in the doorway, cowboy hat in hand. He looked as though he was visiting his grandparents on a Sunday afternoon.

'Karis,' he said nervously after a little while, 'I think we oughta go. My room's right next door.'

Karis strolled across and took hold of him by the bootlace tie. 'Is it now? Well, the bed in here is a bit busy, I guess.' She glanced back at Amelia and winked. 'Come on, Amelia, Ricky has invited us to go next door.'

He looked puzzled. 'Amelia's coming too?'

'Of course, dear Ricky, of course.'

In Ricky's room the narrow bed was flanked by two hard-backed chairs. Karis and Amelia pulled them out into the centre of the floor and sat upon them facing their companion. Ricky perched daintily on the end of the bed. Karis filled tumblers with whisky and ice from the mini-bar and handed them round. Ricky sipped his drink like a man condemned.

'Are you OK?' Karis asked him, full of faux concern, aware that even the way she and Amelia had positioned their chairs was designed to intimidate him. 'You look kinda scared.'

'Scared?' said Ricky in a little voice. 'Why should I be scared?'

'I don't know. I mean, it's not as though Amelia and I are going to touch you . . . or anything. You know, Ricky, we would just be happy to sit here all night and look at you. Being such a pretty boy, as you are.'

Amelia looked at her knees to suppress a loud outburst of laughter. Suddenly she knew only too well what was coming next, remembering the night at college when they had talked the butch football captain, Jim Fuller, into a bag of frazzled nerves.

'I bet you look even better underneath that lovely shirt,' Karis began.

Ricky flicked at his fringe.

'Don't you think so, Amelia?'

'I do, Karis, I do.'

'How about if we ask him nicely to take it off?'

'Take your shirt off, Ricky,' Amelia commanded with an executioner's tone.

Ricky was surprised by the uncompromising sound of the sweet one's voice. 'Aw, c'mon,' he said with a trembling laugh. 'You girls call that asking nicely?'

'Take your shirt off, Ricky,' Amelia repeated. There was still no hint of humour in her voice.

A look of panic flashed in Ricky's eyes. He licked his dry lips. What were they playing at? Did they both want him? Both of them? At once? Oh no. What if he couldn't get it up twice in a row? This was his dream and nightmare all at the same time.

'Is this going to be a threesome?' he asked hopefully, fearfully.

'Don't you know how to undo buttons or something?' Karis deftly avoided his question.

Yeah, thought Ricky, these girls want a kinky threesome. And I'm going to be at the centre of this all-girl sandwich.

'We're waiting,' said Karis.

Ricky's hand flew enthusiastically to the bootlace tie around his neck and he began to frantically tug it loose. Karis rolled her Egyptian-painted eyes. 'Oh, Ricky, Ricky, don't you know that half the joy of the present is in the unwrapping? Slowly, please. Take it a little more slowly.'

He slowed his pace immediately, undoing the pearlised buttons of his white shirt like a pro. Karis leant back in her uncomfortable chair, her fingers steepled in front of her mouth in the gesture that so many men had used during the humiliating casting sessions of her short-lived modelling career. She tapped her fingers thoughtfully against her lips. Ricky slid his arms out of their sleeves and let the shirt fall onto the bed beside him.

'You had better fold that up,' said Amelia, passionlessly.

Playing the game, Ricky did as he was told and sat up straight on the end of the bed, obviously wanting to make a good impression. His arms were tensed, his muscles crossed by veins which bulged in the heat. He had a tattoo of a cowboy's coiled rope on his left bicep and another of a swallow on the right side of his chest, simply outlined in blue ink. Karis and Amelia took the measure of his well-formed pecs, smiled at each other, but said nothing to him.

'Trousers,' Karis announced next. 'No, hang on, hang on,' she said as Ricky's hands flew to his leather belt. 'On second thoughts I think you had better start with your boots.'

Ricky bent down and rolled up the bottoms of his jeans until his snakeskin-detailed, Cuban-heeled cowboy boots were fully exposed. First he grasped the left one by the heel and began to tug it off. He strained and grunted. It was obviously a snug fit. No wonder Bud hadn't bothered with taking his off, Amelia observed. Beneath the boots Ricky was wearing white towelling socks. Karis grimaced. 'And those . . . quickly,' she added, indicating the offending items of clothing with a little wave of her fingers. Amelia bit the knuckles of her hand in an attempt to keep a straight face.

Ricky was breathing quite heavily already. His dark brown chest was covered with a slick sheen of sweat – from the heat of the room, the anticipation of his next order, or the exertion of pulling his boots off? The girls didn't really care.

109

Amelia rocked her chair back onto two legs. Karis lit up a Marlboro cigarette and let the smoke spiral lazily up to the ceiling fan.

Ricky shifted from one bare foot to the other, awaiting his next instructions.

'Now your trousers,' Amelia said.

Ricky stood up and took hold of his buckle.

'Do it nicely, though, eh?'

Ricky's eyes narrowed. Who did these two broads think they were? He hesitated, then dared to ask, 'Hey, ladies, let's just wait a minute. Am I the only one round here who is going to take his clothes off?'

'If you get it wrong, then yes, Ricky, you will be,' Karis said without a hint of a smile. Ricky looked to Amelia for an explanation or reassurance. She was trying to remain implacable but her lips were curved upwards in spite of herself. Of course they would get their clothes off too, Ricky assured himself. They just wanted to play a little game, that's all. Make like it was they who were in control of this situation. He had better let them have their fun if he wanted his. Boy, Ricky thought, if only Bud knew what he was missing.

'Trousers,' Karis repeated. Ricky undid his buckle, pulled off his thick brown leather belt and slowly rolled it up into a tight little coil.

'That's better,' Amelia murmured.

Ricky paused before carrying on, as if he had finally grasped the concept of dramatic effect. He hooked his thumbs in the waistband of his jeans. Karis was looking at a couple of smoke rings she had just puffed into the air. He waited for her to return her attention to him.

'Carry on,' said Karis suddenly.

Amelia crossed her legs as Ricky began to loosen his fly. She tensed her thighs so that they pressed hard, one against the other, gently squeezing her pussy between. Ricky was a pretty fit guy. His chest was broad enough for both her and Karis to lay their heads on. His stomach muscles looked as though they would be able to deflect a speeding bullet. Amelia imagined the strong, brown hands which were unfastening the final silver button of his fly doing the same for her and let out a shivery sigh. Karis gave a look of disapproval.

'Pull them down,' Karis ordered. 'Slowly.'

Ricky began to inch the jeans down over his narrow hips, revealing a pair of pristine white shorts. To the girls' delight, the shorts were already slightly tented around a hard-on at the front. Amelia noticed that Ricky's erection veered slightly to the left. Soon his jeans were by his ankles. Ricky sat back on the bed to pull them free of his feet. They were hard work, a little narrow. As he crossed one leg over the other to help him get the trousers off, Amelia had a sudden view up the right leg of his boxers. The familiar orb of a testicle peeked out from the sparkling cotton. She wanted to reach out and touch it, to feel his balls hot and heavy in the palm of her hand. But she knew she couldn't, at least not yet. This game was all about the agony of not being touched.

'And last but not least, your shorts, please, cowboy,' Karis trilled.

Ricky crossed his arms over his chest, the expression on his face now the cocky look of a guy who knows that he has what just about every girl wants. 'Now c'mon, ladies,' he protested once more. 'I really don't think that this little game of yours is fair.'

'Life isn't fair, Ricky,' Karis replied.

Amelia giggled into her hand.

'And you wouldn't want to blow your chances of being the boss later on, now, would you?'

Amelia felt for the poor underdog in front of her. That last question really was unfair. Ricky stood up one more time and took hold of his shorts.

'Are you ready for this?' he asked proudly. Karis snorted derisively in reply.

Ricky composed himself and whipped the boxers down.

'Ta daa.' Ricky waved his pants theatrically through the air.

'Whoah!' Amelia couldn't stop herself from exclaiming at the sight of Ricky's penis suddenly bursting free from its confines and springing out in front of him. It wasn't as wide as Bud's, but it was longer, smoother. His balls swung below the pink silken shaft in perfect symmetry. He hadn't been circumcised, as most American guys were, and Amelia was glad, because it would make the next part of the game a little easier for him, assuming that Karis wasn't in the habit of carrying a pot of grease in her bag.

Ricky stood before them, naked but proud. His hardening grey eyes challenged them to comment.

'So,' said Karis finally and as breezily as she could in the circumstances. 'Now we know the equipment is all there . . . But,' she continued, 'I would never buy a car just because I liked the colour. I go for a test drive because I like to see it in action. Don't you, Amelia?' Amelia nodded. 'So, Ricky,' she exhaled slowly. 'Let's see you in action.'

'What do you mean?' He looked hopeful. He was obviously thinking that he was going to get to try Amelia out first.

Karis smiled.

'I mean pull your pud, boy. Masturbate. Jack yourself off.'

The shock and silence in the room was palpable. What she had just asked for, he just wasn't prepared to do. No way, José. He never did that. Well, he never did that in front of a girl or in front of anyone for that matter. One of them should do it for him. He stood his ground. He refused. His dick still stuck straight out in front of him. It was obviously game even if he wasn't.

'I ain't going to touch myself for nobody!' he protested.

'He's shy,' Karis mocked.

'Very shy,' Amelia agreed.

'No,' said Karis slyly, 'perhaps he's not shy. I think he's actually just afraid that he won't be able to perform.'

'I . . . I . . .'

113

'Would you like some music to help get you into the mood?' Karis flicked on the television and found MTV. A slinky soul singer was extolling the virtues of anonymous sex. Amelia tapped her foot to the rhythm. Ricky stood stock-still, his eyebrows knitted together in anger.

'You're dickin' me around,' he said, reaching down to the floor to retrieve his discarded shorts. 'I ain't going to stand for this . . .'

'You could sit down for it if you wanted,' quipped Amelia.

'Go to hell.'

Karis fumbled in her handbag for a moment, then, suddenly, a very different light was thrown on the whole scene. In her hand she held something with a long, black barrel. It was covered with a handkerchief, but Ricky knew instantly that it was a gun. It was a gun and she was pointing it right at him. Right at his proud, hard, handsome dick.

Amelia was open-mouthed with horror.

'Karis,' she breathed in disbelief.

'Karis,' sobbed Ricky. His hard-on wavered, just a little.

'Shall I turn the music up?' Karis asked, 'so that nobody outside can hear what is going on?'

There was a moment of interminable stillness and silence before Ricky, shaking like a leaf from head to toe, took hold of his fast-fading dick.

'Are you ready to play the game again?'

Ricky nodded, his chin wobbling. He wrapped one hand loosely around the shaft, his other hand gently cupped his balls. Carefully and with great reverence, he pulled the foreskin back. His deep pink glans was already lubricated and shiny with pre-come. Karis settled back in her seat, the thing in her hand still aimed between Ricky's quivering legs. Amelia, white-knuckled, gripped the arms of her chair.

'Faster, Ricky. We don't have all day.'

There was no point arguing with the black-haired broad now. Gradually, Ricky began to quicken his movements. His hand slicked faster and faster back and forth. He had his eyes fixed on Karis, on the gun in her hand. How the hell was he supposed to concentrate on getting to orgasm when some madwoman might blow his balls off if he got it wrong?

'Relax,' Karis hissed, seeing Ricky struggling with a limp tool. 'You'll find it feels much better.' That was easy for her to say. He couldn't get a hard-on again while he thought about that gun. The blood was draining from his whole body, not just his dick. Karis sighed impatiently. Ricky was sure he saw her thumb shift on the veiled catch.

'Please, no,' Ricky begged. 'Please. Please.'

Karis smiled weakly. Amelia opened her mouth to implore her friend to stop the torment but her words were answered by an increase in the television volume. Ricky screwed his eyes tightly shut against the rest of the room. His only chance was to think of something else. Someone else. He tried to remember Mary-Lou, his high-school sweetheart, in the back of his first car. But all he could see in his mind's eye was the gun in Karis's hand. Where was Bud when he needed him? Perhaps they'd already drugged him and he wasn't asleep next door but in a coma. Of all the girls in Las Vegas, why did he have to run into Thelma and Louise?

'This is getting boring . . .' Karis said in a strange monotone voice even Amelia didn't recognise. Ricky heard the click of the catch. Only an orgasm stood between him and certain oblivion. Mary-Lou, Mary-Lou, he whispered beneath his breath. At last he remembered her little white lace bra. Her polka-dot pink panties. The first nipples he had ever kissed.

'Please, please,' he begged his dormant member. 'Please, please, please.' The music changed to something faster. He blocked out the room, blocked out the maniac woman with her revolver. Pulses of green and purple light flashed before his closed eyes. At last his penis began to rise majestically, though it was taking more effort than for the Ancient Egyptians to raise an obelisk to the sun.

His whole body was growing tense. The outline of his fine muscles was growing clearer. The veins in his forearms were as pumped up as the veins in his dick. Sweat glistened on his clean-shaven upper lip.

His hips bucked forward involuntarily. His eyes were closed now, he was lost to the rhythm of his own actions upon his body. Feeling the rush of steaming blood from his head to his heroic hard-on. Ricky staggered back towards the bed and collapsed down onto the orange candlewick bedspread, still stroking all the while.

He threw his head back, his mouth open in fearful ecstasy. The veins in his neck pulsed as his heartbeat raced faster, ever faster, in time with his hand. He was grimacing now, biting his bottom lip. Preparing for the climax. Enduring the final build-up of the flood before it burst through the dam.

Amelia shifted nervously in her chair. Was he aiming at her?

'Jeez!' Ricky cried, but he wasn't quite there. 'Please, please, please.' The muscles of his stomach contracted painfully, tensing harder and harder, twisting his body up. He wanted to say something but could only splutter now through his broken breathing.

'He's coming, he's coming!' said Karis excitedly, knowing that the sound of her encouraging voice might just give him the tip he needed over the edge.

Ricky strained, still pumping his dick as though he was bringing oil from the bottom of the North Sea. His eyebrows were knitted together in joyful pain. His toes scrunched. Every part of his body was crying out for this ordeal to come to an end . . .

'Oh!'
'Oh!'
'Oh!'

Karis and Amelia both jerked back in their seats

as the first ribbon of sperm shot sky-high, arcing like the jet of a fountain before it fell again and splattered, half across Ricky's thighs, half across the bed. Then another, and another, and another. Each incredible spurt going only a little less high than the one before it. Amelia was open-mouthed with amazement at the incredible volume of his ejaculation. He couldn't have come for a week or more. Ricky let go of his penis. It continued to spurt, jumping about like the end of an unattended hose. He, too, seemed amazed by the intensity of his orgasm. The look on his face suggested that he was just about to pass out.

'Oh, Jeez, no.' He fell backwards onto the bed. His dick stood proudly upright for only a moment or so longer before it began to droop slowly back onto his stomach. Amelia gave a long, low whistle and Karis ran a trembling hand through her long black hair.

When he had recovered from his exertions, Ricky sat up and looked at his mistresses. He was still alive and he had an uncertain smile on his handsome face.

'Well,' he said, looking nervously from one girl to the other in anticipation. 'I did OK, yeah?'

'OK,' Karis agreed.

'So, you two are next?'

'What?' said Karis, already getting to her feet, still pointing her weapon at his crotch as she motioned to Amelia that it was time for them to make an exit.

118

'We're going to get down to real business now, yeah?'

Karis spat out a spiteful laugh. 'Dream on, you jerk-off.' She picked up his cowboy hat, which had been sitting on the dresser and threw it towards him. 'Here, cover yourself up.'

And with that, they were out of the door.

Chapter Ten

'JESUS, KARIS!' AMELIA screamed when they had stopped running from the scene of their latest crime. 'What did you want to get a gun out for? He thought you were going to kill him! *I* thought you were going to kill him! We are going to be in deep shit now. What if he calls the police?'

'Calm down,' Karis told her hysterical friend. 'He loved it.'

'Loved it? Loved it? Karis, you just held a gun to a guy's dick! We could go to jail . . .'

'Here, catch!' Karis tossed the offending weapon, still wrapped in the handkerchief, across to her friend. Amelia bounced it about in her fingers.

'I don't want to get my fingerprints on it!' Amelia squealed. Karis grabbed it back from her.

'Look, stupid.' She threw away the handkerchief. 'Do you really think I would kill a man to see him beat off?' There in the palm of her hand lay, not a gun, but a shiny black and gold vibrator. Karis set it upright in her palm and switched it on. It buzzed around in a little circle.

The tension escaped Amelia's body like a sigh and she collapsed, laughing, against a car-park wall.

'So you can quit worrying now,' said Karis. 'And anyway, what do you think he's going to do, call the cops and say "Officer, officer, two broads just held me up with a dildo?" ... Maybe we should try a bank as well.'

'Maybe we should have got Ricky to do some more,' Amelia sighed as Karis escorted her across the car-park and back through the brightly lit streets of Las Vegas to the Luxor. 'He was amazing, Karis. We should have made the most of him while we had the chance.'

'Oh, quit complaining, Amelia. You already got a screw tonight. I didn't. Besides, I was getting rather bored in there. Every second guy in California looks like him.

'Yeah, but we're in Nevada now, and I don't see us finding another one like that tonight.'

'I'm tired,' said Karis, a little irritably. 'Let's just go to bed.'

'Did you book a room somewhere?'

'I thought I'd stay with you.'

Amelia smiled. Karis wasn't tired.

'Do you mind?'

'I guess not.'

They ascended in the elevator to Amelia's room with their arms linked around each other's waists.

When the door opened at the seventh floor an old lady who was waiting to go down again smiled at them benevolently. She knew that her eyesight was getting bad but she just couldn't tell these days which one of the young couple was the boy. Karis pinched Amelia's bum as they sashayed down the corridor, forcing her to give an outraged shriek. The old lady nodded happily. Young love.

'You are unbelievable, Karis. What will that old lady think?'

'Ah, she'll be dead by the time the elevator reaches the ground floor. Do you have your keys?'

Amelia produced her keys from her pocket and jangled them for effect. Once inside the room, Karis kicked her high heels off straight away and sat down on the end of the bed to massage her toes.

'It's a hard life being a dominatrix,' she moaned.

'Can't you be a dominatrix in flat shoes?' asked Amelia.

'Don't nag me, Miss Sensible. Get me a drink and then come over here. I want you to massage my feet. You're good at it.'

'I haven't done it for a while.'

'Then you need to practise.'

Grudgingly, Amelia knelt at the bottom of the bed and took Karis's right foot in her hands. She rubbed at it fiercely to begin with, to get the circulation going, then she started to work methodically over just a little area at a time. The base of her heel, the outside edge. Karis lay back on the pillows and sighed in ecstasy.

'Do you like that?' Amelia asked.

'I'll say. Isn't that the part of the foot that's directly connected to the sexual organs . . .?'

'No,' said Amelia matter-of-factly. 'That's this bit.' She squeezed another part of Karis's sole at which Karis squealed in pain and pulled her foot quickly out of the way.

'What did you do that for?' she asked.

'Do what?'

'That hurt.'

'Well, according to the ancient art of Chinese foot-massage, that must mean there's something wrong with the corresponding part of your body.'

'Like what?' Karis asked furiously.

'Over-work?'

'You bitch!' Karis swiped at Amelia's head with one of the bright white pillows. Amelia ducked below the end of the bed and the pillow made contact with nothing but air. 'You just better retract that comment, or I'll sue.'

'You can't sue someone for telling the truth.' Amelia continued to dodge the blows.

'I only wish it were. Hell, I was practically a virgin for the whole of last year!' Karis said between swipes. 'I only slept with four or five guys. Six at the very most.'

'Yeah,' Amelia laughed, enjoying the wind-up, 'but that was just the guys. What about the girls?'

'Girls? There's been no one since you.' Out of breath, Karis abruptly gave up the fight.

'Really?' Amelia was suddenly serious. She crawled up from her trench at the bottom of the bed. 'You haven't slept with another girl since me?'

'I haven't slept with another girl ever, as a matter of fact. You were different. You know that.'

Amelia sat down beside her. 'Same for me too.'

'Truly?'

Amelia nodded.

The air between them had become unbearably tense. They looked at each other questioningly until Karis slung an arm around Amelia's neck and laid a friendly kiss on her forehead. Amelia returned the embrace and they stayed locked in a hug for a moment or two.

'Did you ever think about it, what happened between us, while I was away?' Amelia asked.

'Did you?' Karis carefully avoided answering her.

'Sometimes.'

'Yeah. Me too.'

Karis smoothed her hand gently up and down Amelia's back, enjoying the friction of the rough cotton against her fingertips. Amelia's head rested lightly on Karis's slim shoulder. She breathed in the perfume of shampoo and cigarette smoke that lingered in the raven curls of Karis's hair. Amelia lifted the veil of black curls out of the way and planted a delicate kiss on the white skin beneath. She thought she heard Karis murmur something in half-hearted protest, a shiver shook

124

her dancer's body, then Amelia felt a hand squeezing her waist in consent.

'I wish you'd . . .' Amelia began.

'Let's talk about it tomorrow,' said Karis. She took Amelia's face in her hands and smoothed her long fringe out of the way. Karis's lips were cool from her iced drink and her tongue was cool too as it snaked its way into Amelia's mouth. Amelia tasted gin and lipstick, something Karis was never without. While the dark-haired girl nuzzled at Amelia's throat, Amelia flicked her own tongue quickly across her lips and gathered the taste of Karis in.

Karis, too, was relishing familiar smells, a familiar taste, as she ran her tongue up Amelia's neck to her ear. With the very tip of her tongue she circled the emerald earring in Amelia's left lobe. Amelia shivered at the sensation and clutched the back of Karis's neck suddenly with her hand. She pulled Karis back so that their lips met once again. The lipstick was almost gone now, smeared between their mouths, but Karis's lips were almost as red beneath her war-paint. Her pupils had dilated so that they seemed to fill her whole eyes. She had an animal look about her. A look of arousal that hadn't been there when they were making the hapless cowboy Ricky disport himself in his shabby hotel room. Then Karis had been playing. This time the excitement was for real.

Karis sat back on her heels while Amelia undid her tight red button-through top. She breathed in deeply as Karis's breasts were revealed, buoyed up by the luxuriously lacy bra beneath. Her nipples were already hard, poking out through the centres of a pair of lacy flowers. Amelia cupped the breasts in her hands and let her thumbs play gently over the stiff little knobs. Karis exhaled with a ripple of joy. Amelia dipped her head and placed a careful kiss where the cleavage began.

'Now you,' Karis whispered. Obediently Amelia let her sweater be pulled over her head for the second time that evening. She had lost her bra in her brief tussle with Bud and was glad to be rid of the light wool which still irritated her bare skin. But Amelia's breasts had no need for the support of a bra now. Swollen with anticipation, they hung before her like two round ripe peaches, begging to be nibbled and kissed. Her pink nipples stood out in sharp contrast against the soft white skin. Karis cupped them in an echo of Amelia's gesture and paid tribute to each nipple with a lingering kiss.

The gentle kiss that she laid on the left nipple was soon to become something deeper. Carefully, Karis sucked the stiff pink bud into her mouth, elongating it until it was between her even teeth. She nipped at it softly, not so hard as to cause pain, but hard enough to make Amelia draw in her breath sharply. Her whole body became focused around that tiny sensitised part of her which was in Karis's warm mouth. Amelia felt as though her whole being was flowing out through her nipple into Karis, like milk.

'Do it harder,' Amelia asked after a while, when

she had grown used to the rhythmic sucking and the initial strength of the sensation was beginning to die down. But Karis moved her attention to the other nipple and began the whole process again. The deserted nipple ached and throbbed as it once again found itself bare in the air-conditioned room. Karis's saliva dried and cooled there until the nipple felt almost freezing. Amelia looked down to where Karis's bobbing curly head obscured one breast from view, then at the other nipple which now looked bigger than it had ever been before.

Karis moaned quietly as she licked and sucked, drawing the hardened nipple in then letting it drag slowly, slowly out across the sharp edge of her teeth. Amelia closed her eyes and reached blindly for Karis's own breasts, still encased in their expensively lacy bra. Amelia groped around Karis's back until she found the clasp that held the bra there. She unfastened it deftly using only one hand. Karis felt her beautiful olive breasts swing heavily forward and knew that they had been freed. She let Amelia's nipple drop from her mouth and straightened herself up to discard the frivolously small black garment altogether. Now Karis and Amelia sat facing each other, naked from the waist up, as they had done four years before on another warm evening in another anonymous room.

'Should we carry on?' Amelia had asked the same question then. Karis just nodded. Amelia ducked her head and greedily took one of the breasts proffered her into her mouth. Karis's skin was so warm and so silky. The girls stretched out side by side and Amelia lay with her head on Karis's chest. She thought she could hear a heart beating, or perhaps it was the sound of her own pulse that was racing in her ears? An exploratory hand wandered lazily along the curve of Amelia's waist to the top of her jeans.

'Can I?' Karis asked as she began to unbuckle Amelia's belt. Amelia answered her question by doing the same thing herself. Soon they were lying totally naked together. Their hands roaming over corresponding curves as if they were engaged in an ancient and beautiful dance.

Karis was the braver of the two and it was her hand that found its way first between her partner's legs. Amelia gave a little gasp of surprise as she felt herself invaded by the other girl's long, thin fingers, stronger and more purposeful than she remembered.

'Open your legs a little more,' Karis instructed. Amelia drew her uppermost leg towards her so that her vagina lay more open to the gentle caress. 'You're wet already,' Karis smiled.

Her shyness almost completely overcome, Amelia decided it was time that she sought out the hidden treasure beneath Karis's curly black pubic hair but Karis quickly pushed the probing fingers away. Amelia moaned in protest, for Karis's fingers were still rubbing diligently at her clit. She wanted to return the exquisite pleasure in some way. But Karis was determined to keep

Amelia's hands away. For the moment, she was completely in charge.

'Lie on your back,' she instructed.

Amelia rolled over lazily, as if in a dream. Karis took a thigh in each hand and spread Amelia's legs widely apart. Then she took Amelia's arms, which lay untidily by her sides, and pulled them out to the corners of the bed until Amelia was arranged like a human star.

'Don't move,' Karis whispered. From the overnight bag she had left at the foot of the bed she flourishingly produced two gloriously bright silk scarves. Gently but firmly taking Amelia's right wrist, she bound it once as if she were binding an injury, then took the flowing loose ends of the scarf and tied them tightly around the top of the bed. Amelia only looked on in wonder, feeling no fear at the impending curtailment of her freedom. Karis repeated the manoeuvre with the other arm, and then with both of Amelia's legs, using Amelia's belt and Karis's lacy bra to tie the long limbs down. Amelia made no protest at all, sensing that Karis would never cause her harm.

'Stay there,' Karis told Amelia as she lay, now totally naked, and open-legged, across the bed. 'Well, I guess you don't really have a choice,' she added with a laugh. She bounded over to the dresser and rifled through her handbag. And returned with the infamous vibrator, whirring menacingly in her hand.

'It's a stick-up!' she giggled. Amelia writhed

129

deliciously in anticipation. Her instinct was to pull her legs together, to protect herself from the approach of such extreme pleasure, but it was impossible now that they were fastened with her own belt and Karis's bra to the corners of the bed.

'Oh no,' Amelia protested weakly. 'Anything but that.'

But Karis was already kneeling on the end of the bed, her eyes narrowed in an expression of mischief. The vibrator buzzed like an angry wasp, eager to give someone a sting. Amelia twisted helplessly in her bonds and closed her eyes as she felt the cold plastic make contact with her skin.

At first, Karis merely ran the quivering phallus up and down the inside of Amelia's thigh. The vibrations seemed to be travelling through Amelia's muscle to her very bones and although the vibrator was nowhere near her vagina, the resonance reached her labia as well, making them swell and part, eager for their share of the attention.

Tantalisingly, Karis moved the buzzing tool from Amelia's right inner thigh to her left, just touching Amelia's aching clit as she passed over it. From time to time, the vibrator touched a couple of her pubic hairs, which transmitted the vibrations along to their roots. Amelia bit her lower lip. Karis was going to make this moment last a lifetime.

'Karis, Karis, stop, please,' Amelia breathed in desperation as the vibrator passed from left to right again, still not touching her throbbing sex.

'This is agony.'

'I know,' Karis laughed.

Unexpectedly, Karis got up from the bed altogether and walked around it and up to where Amelia's head lay on its pillow, rolling distractedly from side to side. Karis leaned over her so that her long black curls brushed lightly against Amelia's cheek. She kissed her. Amelia responded as though Karis's mouth was a succulent ripe strawberry and she hadn't eaten for days. The vibrator still buzzed in Karis's hand, touching Amelia's ribs and making her shiver as Karis kissed her a little harder. All too soon, Karis sat up again and began to play the quivering head of her hand-held toy up and down Amelia's naked torso.

Around Amelia's nipples, Karis worked the buzzing head. The little pink buds strained upwards, reaching that point where they became so sensitive that pleasure was almost replaced by pain. Amelia bit her lower lip harder still between her straight white teeth. She didn't want to cry out, to let Karis know that she was winning and could do anything she wanted to this body tied down before her now. Karis lazily trailed the vibrator down between the breasts and across Amelia's gently curved stomach. She danced it gaily around Amelia's belly button and carried on down until, once again, she was at Amelia's pubic hair.

'No,' Amelia groaned. But no wasn't what she meant at that moment.

Karis smiled wickedly. She resumed her position between Amelia's open legs, without once breaking contact between the vibrator and her flesh. The vibrator hovered at the edge of Amelia's mound like a sacrificial dagger, waiting to plunge deep inside her and take her out of this room to somewhere altogether more exciting and ecstatic. The few seconds that the vibrator took to inch down, through the hair, towards Amelia's desperate clit seemed like a thousand lifetimes. Amelia felt as though she was holding her breath, coming up from the bottom of a deep, deep lake. Waiting, longing to exhale again.

Then, finally, it was there. The sensation exploded through Amelia's body, rushing up from her clitoris like a flame along a gunpowder trail. The vibrations, which were so frenzied and frenetic at their point of entry into her, were spreading out as far as her head like the circles which surround a stone dropped into a pool. Amelia's hands were clenched into fists, her ankles twisted in their bindings as Karis dropped the vibrator a little more again, bringing it onto the pouting lips of her vagina, finding a way between them into the narrow passage that was longing to allow her in. The vibrator slipped easily inside, sliding effortlessly in and out of the wet juices that heralded Amelia's enjoyment and desire. In the distant blur of sight and sound that the room had become, Amelia heard the flicking of a switch and felt the vibrator move up to another level of power. Karis might as well have connected her lover straight to the mains.

Amelia's hips writhed skywards until Karis had to hold her still in order to continue the torturous pleasure she wanted to inflict. Alternately plunging the vibrator into Amelia's vagina and then pulling it out to dance it over her clit, Karis laughed as she worked. Her own arousal was building inside her unfettered body. She felt supremely sensitive. She could feel the gentle brush of her black curls on her shoulders as she moved. The vibrator in her hand was sending waves up her arms so that she felt somehow plugged in to the body on the bed, sharing the experience. As Amelia panted and strained against her bindings, it finally became too much for Karis to maintain her own calm demeanour. With one hand, she held the vibrator against Amelia's clit, with the other, she sought out her own and pressed hard against the tiny throbbing nerve-head.

'Karis, Karis,' Amelia squealed.

But Karis could not hear. Though she felt close to Amelia, she was at the same time very far away, cocooned in her own pleasure. Suddenly she ripped the vibrator away from Amelia and plunged it, still wet with her friend's juices, into her own vagina. Kneeling on the bed, she drew herself up and then flopped back down again between Amelia's open legs. She curled her body up and then straightened out as the spasms began to wrack her body. Amelia, left unattended, continued to pant. She had already reached a point of no turning back and the sight of her torturess in the throes of her own orgasm kept Amelia's climax at boiling point.

'Oh, oh, ohhh . . .' Karis screamed in ecstasy to the ceiling. Her entire body hovered momentarily in an upright position before she collapsed back on to the mattress, and from there slid, like a drowning girl going under, onto the thick cream-carpeted floor.

When all had gone quiet again, Amelia suddenly became aware that she was still bound to the bed like a beached starfish. Karis lay on the floor, motionless except for the gentle heaving of her delicate ribcage. It looked suspiciously as though she had fallen asleep.

'Karis,' Amelia called softly. 'Karis, are you asleep?'

There was no answer from the prone body on the carpet.

'Typical,' thought Amelia. 'And I thought it was just men who rolled over and fell asleep.'

Fortunately for Amelia, Karis did come round again before the bindings had completely cut off the blood supply to her feet and hands. Free to move now, Amelia stretched out an arm and turned off the light. Karis was curled into her side, her head resting on Amelia's shoulder, her raven hair spread out across Amelia's smooth white skin like a lacy veil. For a moment in the darkness they lay still in silence, but both were aware that the other was not about to go to sleep just yet.

'Amelia,' Karis piped up first, 'I wish you didn't have to go so soon.'

'I know,' said Amelia. 'So do I.'

But there was to be no change to Amelia's plans this time. The next afternoon she got Karis to drive her to the airport and resisted all attempts to make her extend her stay for just another day.

'Final call for flight LH042.'

Amelia glanced at her watch.

'Look, Karis, I've really got to go.' She started to get to her feet and gather up her hand luggage.

'You'll be back soon, yes?' Karis asked. 'For my wedding?'

'For your wedding! Karis, I might never come back if I wait for someone to make an honest woman of you. Besides, it's your turn to visit me.'

'Oh yeah,' groaned Karis. 'Only when London gets hot . . . or hell freezes over.'

They shared a final hug. Amelia broke away first. Karis was dabbing at the corner of one eye. 'Get going, girl,' she told her old friend, 'before my false lashes get washed off.'

'We'll be in touch again soon, Karis,' Amelia assured her, neither of them knowing that it might be much sooner than they both expected.

Chapter Eleven

AS SOON AS Amelia found her seat in the body of the plane, she rifled through the in-flight bag for the complimentary eye-mask and slipped it on. Then she lay back and made an effort to go to sleep. After her ill-timed nap, Karis had kept Amelia awake for most of the night, making love to her and talking about old times and the bright futures they were planning. Amelia was glad that Karis had managed to find her in Las Vegas. At one stage she had thought that they might never see each other again, after the embarrassment of their confused affair at college. Amelia wouldn't let their friendship lapse so far again.

Right up until the very last moment, it appeared as if Amelia was going to have her row of three seats entirely to herself. She was looking forward to spreading herself out across them soon after take-off when, to her disappointment, she was joined by a young guy who looked as though he had been running to get there on time. A·stewardess helped him to cram his bulky hand luggage into the overhead locker and fastened his seat-belt for him. He was the last person to board the plane.

'Henry,' he said in a cut-glass English accent as he offered Amelia his hand. The stewardess had asked Amelia to remove her eye-mask for the duration of the safety video.

'Amelia,' she replied, taking the proffered hand politely. Why did she always have to sit next to someone who wanted to talk when all she needed was to spend the entire flight asleep?

'Can't wait until we're allowed to smoke,' Henry said nervously. 'Calms the nerves, you know.'

'I think you'll find that this is the no-smoking section,' replied Amelia dryly.

'Oh, damn . . .' Henry swore. 'Oh, sorry, shouldn't swear in front of a lady. Sorry.'

Amelia smiled and pulled her mask down to cover her eyes again. Henry was cute, in a floppy-fringed public schoolboy kind of way. She wondered how old he was. No doubt he would let her know later.

'Flying back to London?' Henry asked.

'Unless we run out of fuel on the way.'

'Oh, yes. Stupid question, I suppose. Though you could be going on to somewhere else.'

'No,' sighed Amelia, 'I'm just flying back to London.'

'Me, too. Back to work tomorrow. Not that I'll

137

be able to get much done with the jet-lag I'll have and all that.'

'No, I don't suppose you will . . . Hey, listen, Henry, I really hate to sound unfriendly, but I've had a long and busy night and I really would appreciate the opportunity to get some sleep right now. Do you mind?' She raised her eye-mask to giving him a pleading look.

'Oh, I am sorry,' Henry bumbled. 'It's just that I get so nervous when I'm flying that I have to talk to take my mind off the fact that I'm sitting in a tube of metal about three hundred miles up in the sky.'

'It's safer than being in a car.'

'Yes, but you're unlikely to have a car crash over the Atlantic.'

'Oh, Jeez,' groaned Amelia, catching sight of his white-knuckled hand gripping the arm-rest between them. 'Look, you just cover yourself up with a blanket, Henry, and let me take your mind off being a mile high . . .'

Henry looked at Amelia quizzically. His big brown eyes blinked rapidly while he waited for her to explain. Amelia licked her lips. On closer inspection he was really very handsome indeed, though a little drained with fear, and perhaps not quite as young as she had at first thought.

'Cover yourself up with a blanket, Henry,' she repeated. 'They'll be turning the lights off soon so that everyone can get some sleep. And then I'll tell you a nice bedtime story.' She casually laid a hand on his knee to underline her intention. If she was going to have to talk to him she was at

138

least going to make sure she had some enjoyment as well.

The stewardesses turned out the lights and made a final journey up and down the plane to check that everyone had all they needed. Henry had unfolded his grey blanket and now it lay across his knees. Amelia was beneath hers too, but her hand had already crept up Henry's legs towards the top of his thigh. His firm thigh muscle had tensed until she was sure it must be feeling painful. Amelia chatted casually about the weather for a while to calm him down until the last stewardess had disappeared into the little staff booth. Then she leant in closely and began to whisper hotly in Henry's reddening ear.

'Are you ready?'

He nodded.

'OK. Then I'll begin. Once upon a time,' she said in a soft, sing-song voice, 'a brave Amazon set out on a journey from her village to find the source of eternal life.' Amelia tiptoed her fingers up Henry's legs beneath the blanket to represent the heroine of her story beginning her quest. 'She had a vague idea of the direction in which the source lay, but to get there she had to cover all sorts of rough and tricky terrain, encountering on her journey all kinds of trial and hardship . . .' Amelia smiled to herself as her fingers wandered blithely over Henry's stiffening member and started off down his other leg. 'But she didn't care how long it took, or what she had to do, because in the end she knew it would be worth it . . .'

Henry sighed deeply and looked at the redhead whose fingers were currently ambling down to his right knee. Their eyes met. Amelia bit her lower lip and winked at Henry in a gesture of shameless flirtation. Suddenly Henry forgot that he was in a metal tube, three hundred miles up. His fluttering heart was already flying higher than that.

'A short while into her epic journey,' Amelia continued, her fingers walking slowly up Henry's blue chambray-clad chest, 'the Amazon came to a sheer rock wall. It was incredibly high and she didn't think she would be able to scale it.' Her fingers slipped languorously down towards Henry's belt. He closed his eyes and inhaled loudly. 'But she got about halfway up by taking a long run at it . . .' Henry exhaled in disappoint- ment as Amelia's fingers raced back up from his navel to the centre of his chest. 'However it soon became clear that there was to be no going over the top and so she had to look for a way through.' The roaming hand moved towards Henry's pearly white buttons.

The blanket was slipping down. Amelia used her free hand to pull it up towards Henry's chin.

'She had to find a way through,' Amelia recapped as she started to twist the first button out of its buttonhole. 'And, luckily for the resourceful Amazon, she was able to use her skills to open an ancient door which someone else had kindly put there before . . .' Amelia's fingers slipped inside Henry's shirt and rested on his hot chest. They rose up and down slowly with his measured breathing.

'Inside the cave she had found it was very dark, and strange wiry stemmed plants grew from the hard, smooth walls.' Amelia's fingers wove their way through the soft hair which grew messily between Henry's nipples. 'Their gentle tendrils wrapped themselves around our heroine's legs and made it difficult for her to walk. She knew that she was far from her goal and by hesitating too long she might lose everything, when, suddenly,' Amelia's fingers made contact with a nipple, 'the Amazon happened upon a curious handle which grew up from the rock beneath her hand.' Amelia's stroking fingers were stiffening the nipple to a hardened point. Henry sighed and kissed Amelia's forehead through her fringe. 'Being a truly brave warrior as she was, the Amazon twisted the handle and found herself falling, falling, thousands of feet through the rock to land on a pile of the softest grass she had ever had the good fortune to fall upon.'

Amelia slid her hand right down Henry's chest and pushed her way past the waistband of his trousers to the top of his pubic hair. 'Now, she just knew that she was getting very warm indeed.'

Henry breathed in. Amelia's fingers slipped a little further beneath his belt until they struck gold. Henry's dick was already semi-hard, only his shyness at being fondled by a complete stranger in such a public setting was tempering what could be an enormously impressive hard-on. Suddenly, Amelia's other hand was beneath Henry's blanket and she was quickly unfastening his thick leather belt.

'Not much room to manoeuvre,' she explained. He looked at her with an expression of shock in his big, blinking eyes.

'I say, Amelia, I don't know if . . .'

'If I should be doing this? Lighten up, Henry. It's less frightening than thinking about flying.'

He wasn't sure about that.

'No one can see. The stewardesses certainly won't bother to come out of their cabin unless they have to. And even if they do, I assure you they've seen it all before.'

Henry gulped. Amelia took hold of the tab of his zip and pulled it down before he could protest. Now she had enough room to put her hand right inside his trousers and get beneath the elastic of his close-fitting briefs. She could imagine what they would look like, and, judging from the rest of his outfit, they would probably be in sensible navy blue.

Henry's dick twitched as the blood rushed from his body to its favourite extremity.

'That's better,' said Amelia. 'Now I can carry on.'

The guy in the seat across the aisle from Henry's let out a tremendous snore.

'See, nobody else is listening. Where was I? Oh, yes, our brave heroine knew that at long last she had come to the right place. But as she looked around her, at the proud monolith that marked the source of eternal life, she noticed that there didn't seem to be all that much life in the area. What was she to do?'

Amelia's fingers curled around the base of Henry's warm, smooth shaft.

'Thank goodness she knew that to bring the elixir from the bottom of the well, there was a great big handle that she would have to find and pull . . .'

Henry bit his lip as the hot hand moved upwards. He saw the blanket move quite discernibly.

'But not too hard, of course . . .'

Amelia's hand travelled back downwards. Henry sucked in his breath sharply and Amelia wondered briefly whether she had just caused him some pain. The anguished look on his face soon dissolved into a beatific smile however, and so she carried on. There was no need to continue with the story now. It had served its purpose and Henry was no longer listening to anything Amelia said anyway. That was a shame, Amelia thought, since she had come up with a great ending for her epic tale, with Henry playing the source of the elixir of life, of course.

As Amelia eased her hand back and forth with a smooth, fast rhythm, she felt the shaft hardening further still beneath her hand. Occasionally it would twitch upwards with impressive force, making her long for a little more leg room and a little less of an audience so that she could climb onto Henry's lap and slip his tremendous length inside. But for now that wasn't possible and so she would have to make do with witnessing his pleasure ... Perhaps not, she smiled to herself. There was something they could do. She let go of Henry's penis suddenly and, before he had time to protest, was quickly pulling up his zip again, having first carefully tucked his turgid dick back behind his fly.

'I'm going to the loo,' she told him. 'There's no queue right now. Give me thirty seconds or so and then you can follow me up there. Knock on the door like this.' She lightly demonstrated a secret knock on the collapsible meal tray which folded down from the seat in front. 'And then I'll let you in.'

Amelia jumped up and strolled nonchalantly down the plane. She ensconced herself in a cubicle and waited. She checked her reflection in the dark mirror. She waited. She fixed her hair a little. She waited. Where was he? She'd said thirty seconds and he had been at least two minutes. The hard-on she had so carefully nurtured would probably be non-existent by now.

Just when she was about to give up hope, there came the secret knock at the door.

Amelia slid the door open just enough to let him inside.

'Where have you been?' she hissed.

'Two seconds after you got up, another passenger decided that he needed to go as well. I had to wait in my seat until there was no queue again.'

'OK. You're forgiven.' She was already unfastening his belt. She had ascertained from the outline of his trousers that all was not completely lost. Once the flies were undone, Amelia pushed Henry's trousers down over his hips to his knees. His briefs came off simultaneously. Amelia couldn't help but let out a tiny laugh when she saw that they were indeed navy blue.

When Henry was ready, his dick standing up proudly in anticipation, Amelia carefully turned around in the tiny space so that she was facing away from him. She put down the toilet seat and stood with one leg on either side of its aluminium bowl. Then she hitched up her skirt and bent over, her hands braced against the wall at the back of the cubicle. Henry's dick nudged at the rose-pink and swollen entrance of her aching sex without her having to move an inch.

'Come on then,' she told him, her voice husky with arousal. 'Give it to me.'

Away from the eyes of the other passengers, Henry was still hesitating. Amelia wondered for a second whether she was being just a little too keen for this shy English boy.

'What if we get caught?' Henry asked.

'We'll be all right as long as you don't have a cigarette afterwards. Get on with it, please, Henry.'

Henry cleared his throat. Amelia closed her eyes and waited for the first thrust. The blood rushed to her head and sent tingles through her entire body as she felt him gently nudging at her labia with his penis, trying to find a way inside. But two false starts were quite enough and soon

145

she was impatiently guiding his shaft between her labia herself, gasping with the joy the feeling of being filled up in such a risky setting gave her.

'That's it. Push right in.'

Feeling behind her, Amelia grasped hold of one of Henry's hands and had him place it on her waist. Then she did the same to the other.

'Rock me backwards onto you,' she instructed in a hoarse whisper. 'Use my waist to pull me towards you.'

Henry did as Amelia told him and soon they were building up a satisfying rhythm with the bare minimum of movement between them. Once or twice, Henry crashed backwards into the metal folding door and Amelia had to stop herself from crying out by using one of her hands as a bit between her teeth. But it was a divine feeling. Being taken from behind was one of Amelia's favourite positions when she had all the time in the world, but here, in the bathroom of an aeroplane, with the added tension of knowing that too much noise or movement would let everyone know what was going on, Amelia didn't know if she would be able to hang on to her orgasm long enough to join Henry as he came.

Fortunately for Amelia, Henry wasn't going to be able to last out for that long either. By twisting her head slightly to the side, Amelia could see both their bodies reflected in the dark glass mirror. Henry had his head thrown back, his mouth open, letting out a small guttural grunt each time he pulled her body towards his. He was transfigured by his pleasure from a boy afraid of flying into some kind of fucking machine. He filled her so perfectly. He was so hard, and hardening ever more as his crisis approached. Amelia felt his shaft jerk upwards as it had done in her hand. His balls slapped against her body, the vibrations to her clitoris giving her so much intense pleasure that she thought her shaking knees might buckle beneath her.

'Yes, yes,' Henry was hissing. 'Yes, yes, I'm going to come.' He drew her body towards his faster and faster, more and more ferociously, so that suddenly he pulled her right away from the wall. Straightening her body up against his, Henry clasped Amelia to him, still pumping into her from behind. Amelia's arms flailed to find something to grasp hold of as their bodies began to buck, both at once. Henry groaned as his hot semen began to shoot deep, deep inside her. His spasms were echoed by the movements of Amelia's pulsating vaginal walls, squeezing and massaging his frenzied dick until the last of his come was pooling inside her and dribbling slowly down her legs.

Amelia and Henry stood locked in their position for a while. Henry breathed raggedly in her ear. She reached up to cup his face and hold his hot cheek against hers. His hands roamed lazily over her breasts.

After a minute or so, Amelia remembered where they were and slowly eased herself away from Henry's sweating loins. She pulled her skirt down hurriedly and set about straightening her hair in the mirror once again. Henry had collapsed backwards against the door where he leant with his eyes closed, still panting like the winner of a long and difficult race. Amelia gave him a playful pinch.

'Henry, Henry,' she called softly. 'Get yourself straightened up. We've got to get back to our seats. I'll go first. Don't forget to act nonchalant.'

Amelia squeezed out past Henry who still didn't seem altogether awake. A middle-aged lady was standing just outside the cubicle. She moved towards the door as Amelia slipped out and was very surprised when it locked again as she tried to get in. Amelia walked quickly back to her seat, trying not to look at the people sitting near to the loos who had probably heard everything that went on. Oh well, thought Amelia, perhaps they hadn't. Henry wasn't what you would call a screamer, she reflected. He was probably too well brought up.

'Still scared of flying?' Amelia asked when Henry finally returned to his seat beside her.

He took up her hand which lay on the arm-rest between them. 'Not at all,' he replied. 'I could make this flight twice a day . . . But I wonder if when we get back to London, you'd like to help me overcome my irrational fear of strange beds?'

'I need some sleep,' Amelia told him, then she covered herself up with a blanket again and left Henry trying to arrange his long body comfortably in his cramped seat.

*

148

The flight landed safely and on time, with Henry gripping Amelia's fingers until they went blue as the plane made its descent. In the customs hall, Amelia's luggage came around on the carousel first. Henry was still standing nervously beside her, obviously wanting to suggest for real that they meet again sometime but being too scared to say when and how. Amelia dragged her heavy blue suitcase off the conveyor and onto the floor. She sat on top of it while she rooted through her hand luggage for a scrap of paper and a pen.

'What's your number, Henry?' she asked.

'Oh, my number . . .' Henry didn't tell her what it was. Instead he fumbled in his jacket pocket and eventually brought out a card. 'It's on there. My mobile number. It's probably more use than giving you the one at home since I'm hardly ever in in the evenings.'

Amelia took the card from his shaking hand without reading it and thanked Henry for his pleasant company on the flight. She would ring, she promised, but for now all she wanted to do was get home. It was while Amelia was finding change for the taxi driver who dropped her off in Kentish Town that Henry's card came into her hand once again. As she waited for Richard to open the front door, Amelia fetched the card out and read it at last.

'Henry Du Pre. Mountain Music A & R.' So he was a talent spotter for Mountain. He hadn't mentioned that. Perhaps, thought Amelia, she would be ringing Henry after all.

Chapter Twelve

FOUR DAYS ALONE with Amelia's cat was enough for any man, thought Richard. Particularly when he had to come home every evening to face not only that mewling menace but a message from arch-ratbag Jamie Nettles on his answer-machine to boot. That guy sounded desperate, crazed even. What had Amelia done to him? Probably the same as she did to me, Richard reflected bitterly. The phone rang, the answer-phone kicked in – Richard had set it to call-screen.

'Richard, darling, it's Amy. I'm at the airport – on my way back. If you're going to go out before I get in, could you remember to leave the key next door. I can't find mine. I missed you. See you later. Bye.' She blew kisses into the receiver. Richard's heart leapt involuntarily. She was coming back. And early.

Now she was here. Richard bounded to the door

and helped her drag her cases up the stairs. She opened her hand luggage and threw him a red baseball cap with 'Las Vegas' embroidered on it in gold thread, 'to hide his bald patch'. Richard took mock offence but was secretly thrilled she had remembered him.

'So, how was your trip?' Richard asked. 'How was the wedding? What was your bridesmaid's dress like? I bet you looked lovely.'

'The trip was tiring. The wedding was pretty much the same as the last one. The dress was Edwardian-style burnt clementine velvet with an ivory skirt and I looked like a monster.'

'You know you didn't,' Richard sighed. 'And the flight back? How was that?'

'Turbulent,' Amelia smiled. She was flipping quickly through the pile of envelopes which had accumulated during her brief absence. 'Any calls?' she asked when her rummage turned up nothing of any significance.

'Yes,' said Richard, his welcoming smile tightening. 'I didn't erase the answer-machine so you can listen to them yourself.'

'Thanks.' Amelia tripped into the lounge straightaway and flicked her messages on. At the sound of Jamie's voice Richard felt sure he saw the corners of her mouth twitch upwards.

'Amy, it's Jamie, Friday night. I've got a window in my diary, do you fancy coming out?'

'Amy, Jamie, Saturday morning. I'm not doing anything this evening so I thought you might like to come and grab a bite to eat with me.'

'Amy, Jamie, Saturday p.m. Have you gone away for the weekend? I hope not. I'm still free tonight . . .'

And so on and so on.

'I suppose I better call him,' Amelia shrugged. She dialled his number, from memory Richard noticed, and got through to the answer-machine at his home. 'Jamie, darling. Sorry, I've been indisposed. Yes, let's get together sometime soon and talk about this contract of mine. That would be nice. Can't wait to see you again.' More kisses down the telephone line.

Richard grimaced. What did that creep Nettles have that he didn't? Apart from blond hair and a great car? He took a deep breath. No point letting Amelia know he was bothered.

'So, what else did you do, apart from go to the wedding?' Richard persisted.

'I spent some time hanging round casinos, bumped into a couple of old friends from college.' Her eyes drifted faraway for a moment and her mouth lifted at the corners in a secret smile. 'Jerry was there too.'

'In Las Vegas?'

'Yes. He's in the States for work.' Amelia looked straight at Richard. He looked as if he already knew which bomb she was about to drop. 'It was a shock to see him there. I nearly scratched his eyes out when I first saw him but we've made it up. I'm getting back together with him.' Richard felt the blood draining from his cheeks, but reminded himself quickly that it wasn't his place to care.

'That's nice,' he forced himself to tell her. 'So, will you be moving out again?'

'I'm not sure . . . yet,' Amelia replied breezily. 'But as soon as I do know, rest assured you will be the first to hear.'

'Great,' said Richard. 'Thanks.'

'In fact,' Amelia continued, 'I think I'll call Jerry right now. Let him know that I had a safe flight home. What time will it be over there?'

Five minutes later, Amelia hung up the phone and dragged herself into the kitchen with the look of a dog that had just been kicked in the face. Richard was making toast. He buttered a slice and stuck it into her hand while he waited for her to decide whether or not he was going to hear about her latest disaster. He could see the tears welling in her eyes as she ate until, suddenly, she let out an almighty blub and a shower of toast crumbs spattered onto the floor.

Richard crammed the rest of his slice of toast into his mouth and rushed to put his arms around her.

'It's not fair,' she sobbed. 'He said he was coming back next week, but now he says he's not.'

'Who?'

'Jerry.'

'Oh.'

'He says he's going to be in LA for another week at the very least and then he may have to go straight from LA to New York for a project that could take months to complete. Months and months and months! What am I supposed to do, Richard? Waiting here in London all on my own?'

All on her own? Richard tried not to be offended. Didn't he and Eliza count as company any more? Amelia wailed into the shoulder of his soft green shirt. This he could do without. But how could he cheer her up? Tell her that Jerry was a rat and she should run away with him instead? That gem of enlightenment hadn't worked last time.

'Hey, cheer up,' he said helpfully after considering the matter for a long while. Then he was struck with something resembling inspiration. 'What you need is something to take your mind off this minor hiccup . . .'

'Minor hiccup?' Now Amelia was offended.

'This great disaster,' Richard continued a little more carefully.

'You're right,' said Amelia, sniffing delicately. 'I should go upstairs and write some more songs. Concentrate on my music for a bit. After all, I've got a meeting with Jamie Nettles soon. He promised me he would have a publishing contract for me by the end of this week.'

Richard pulled a strange, doubtful face.

'What are you looking at me like that for?' Amelia asked.

'Well,' Richard took a deep breath, 'I don't know whether I ought to say this, but . . .' There was never going to be a right time for what Richard was about to reveal to her next.

154

'But what? Go on, Richard,' Amelia snapped belligerently. 'Make my day.'

'It's just that I don't think you should bother with Jamie Nettles any more. You know that he works at the same company as me . . .'

'Go on.' Amelia was beginning to look frightening.

'Well, the other day, I was in the canteen and he happened to come and sit next to me for lunch. We have a vague acquaintanceship . . . He calls me "Dick". Anyway, we got talking about the projects he's working on at the moment and your name came up . . .'

Amelia paled. 'And?'

'And it seems that he's not really interested in your music at all, Amelia. He told me that he is just stringing you along with the promise of a contract because he's after your body.'

'No, no, no! That's just idle, jealous, gossip!' screamed Amelia, going from white to red, but the potential for the truth in Richard's words had already hit home. She started to cry again. Richard fluttered around her with a box of tissues while Amelia muttered vague death threats to the male population in general and Jamie Nettles in particular.

'Hey Amelia, calm down. Calm down. Listen, I've been invited to a party tonight. It's my cousin's engagement party actually. You should come along too. It might not be exactly your kind of scene. Plenty of maiden aunts. No hard drugs to speak of.' Amelia frowned at that aspersion.

'But we might have a really good time. There'll be lots of music and dancing!'

'Where is it?' she asked suspiciously.

'In a village just outside Oxford. I'll drive. And we can leave the minute you start to get bored.'

'OK,' she sniffed. 'Then I'll come.'

Richard was surprised that she agreed so quickly and mentally rubbed his hands together with glee. He was going to spend the evening with Amelia and at the very least that meant that he wouldn't have to put up with his grandmother asking him why he wasn't 'courting' all night.

The party sucked, as Richard knew it would, but hadn't let on to Amelia. It was held in a draughty church hall, which was festooned for the occasion with plenty of balloons printed 'Congratulations'. Amelia chatted politely with Richard's grandmother and listened to stories about his childhood. It was obvious that she thought Richard and Amelia were together, and Amelia didn't tell her otherwise, much to Richard's relief. In fact, when the DJ announced the final song of the evening, Amelia was the first to her feet, pulling Richard with his two left feet out onto the floor for the last dance.

'Richard,' Amelia whispered seductively as they swayed slowly to the rhythm. He waited with butterflies dancing madly around his stomach for her to continue. The touch of her breath on his ear and the proximity of her body in its thin, cotton jersey dress was giving him a hard-on already. 'Richard, I'm sorry about earlier on. I really am grateful for what you told me about that snake, Jamie Nettles. You're a great house mate, you know that.'

Oh well, it was better than nothing. Halfway through the song a distant cousin of Richard's strolled casually over and dragged Amelia from his arms. Richard stood at the side of the dance-floor, waiting for the song to finish, watching her drift lazily around in Mitchell's lecherous grip. Her eyes were faraway. He wondered what she was thinking about. Him? Probably not.

Richard's grandmother suddenly pulled on his sleeve.

'That's a lovely girl you've got there, Dicky,' she said.

Yes, Amelia was a lovely girl, but he hadn't got her, not yet.

Held in a church hall as it was, the party finished long before midnight. In the car-park, Amelia waited patiently while Richard warmed up his old car to the point where it would actually start. It was a balmy August night. The sky was clear and, away from the constant glow of the artificial light of London, they were actually able to see the stars.

There was a strange, spluttering sound. Richard's car had started.

'Are we driving straight back?' Amelia asked as she climbed into the passenger seat.

'If you want to.'

'Not really. It's not that late and I like being out here in the country. Is there anywhere we can go to look at the stars?'

Richard was only too happy to oblige.

Not far from the village where the party had been held stood an ancient monument known as the Rollright Stones. It was a symbolic circle of stones, nowhere near as big or impressive as Stonehenge but just as old. Legend had it that no one had ever been able to count the number of stones correctly. That every time you counted them up the number you came to would be different. Richard had even heard a story about a camera which was ripped out of its owner's hands and whipped up into the sky by a freak wind when he tried to take a photograph of this mystical place. Richard parked the car on the road between the main circle and the King Stone which stood alone in another field. He helped Amelia over the rusted iron fence.

'Wow, just feel the vibes,' Amelia laughed when she stood in the centre of the moonlit ring. She spun around, arms open like a whirling dervish. Richard sat down on the ground beside her. He picked out a juicy blade of grass and bit upon it ruminatively. The stones looked out across a vista of rolling fields which were silver and blue in the glittering moonlight. Amelia lowered herself tentatively to sit beside him.

'The grass is damp,' she explained.

'No, it's not. But you can sit on my jacket if you like.' Richard lay flat out and gazed at the sky. Using his grass as a pointer, he drew her attention to a cluster of stars.

'That's the Great Plough.'

'Is it really?'

Richard nodded solemnly. 'And that's the Milky Way. That's Pisces, that's Aries and that's Uranus.'

'Wow,' said Amelia, her mouth open in awe as she took it all in. 'How do you know all this stuff about the stars?'

'I don't,' replied Richard. 'I was making it all up.'

'You monster!' exclaimed Amelia. She leant over his body, hands on either side of his shoulders, to pull a face at him. But before she could right herself again, Richard stopped her where she was, holding her tightly just above the elbows. His eyes locked with hers provocatively. The wind rippled the grass around his head so that it looked almost as though they were lying in water.

'Kiss me,' he said.

Amelia's eyes flickered nervously across his face. Richard held his gaze steady on her soft lips. He had called her bluff, but just as he thought she would refuse and pull away, she bent her elbows and dipped gracefully down to meet his upturned mouth. And she stayed there.

They kissed softly, gently. Sometimes her lips seemed merely to graze his. Gradually, Amelia shifted her body until she lay on top of Richard, her legs either side of his legs, her toes pressing against the ground, her hands knitted together in his short, tousled hair. Richard pushed his tongue carefully between her even white teeth. She responded in kind. He traced the well-defined cupid's bow of her lips with the tip of his tongue.

Carefully, Richard rolled over so that now Amelia was on the grass and he was on top of her. She laughed up at him. Her big eyes glinted darkly with the reflected light of the full moon. He studied her reverently for a moment, as though she were a painting, until Amelia felt freaked out by his staring and insisted that he continue to kiss her, and with his eyes shut at that.

Her hands were in his hair again, caressing the back of his head, then his ears, then tracing along the stubbly line of his jaw with her fingertips. They rolled onto their sides so that Richard no longer had to support himself with his hands but could use them instead to rove all over her. Amelia had untucked his grey marl T-shirt from the waistband of his jeans and her fingers were now softly moving over his warm bare skin. She lingered on a tiny raised mole. Her touch was so light at times that it almost tickled.

Amelia was wearing a floral printed dress that fastened all the way down the front with tiny, mother of pearl buttons. Her familiar amber pendant hung from a slightly shorter chain around her throat. Richard began to fumble with

160

the buttons nearest the scoop neck of the dress but they were fragile and he found them difficult to budge from the fabric loops into which they were hooked for fear of breaking them. Sensing his nervousness, Amelia flopped onto her back and began to help him set her free, giggling. Soon her dress was open to reveal her flimsy cotton all-in-one, which was also printed with roses. Richard sighed impatiently when he saw that he had to breach another layer of resistance before he could reach her smooth skin. Amelia meanwhile had gone straight for his fly and was manhandling his dick out through the slit in his boxer shorts.

'I don't want to take my dress off. I'll get a rash from the grass,' she told him matter-of-factly when he tried to push the dress from her shoulders.

'But how . . .?' he started to protest.

'It's got poppers,' she told him, indicating the crotch of her lacy all-in-one. He heard a faint popping sound as she undid the first one herself, then the second, and the third. Amelia wriggled the clingy material up around her hips until her venus mound was completely exposed to the glittering sky. Richard smiled. He took her hips in his hands as if they were the handles of a holy grail and brought her pelvis up to meet his descending mouth. He placed a first kiss just below her belly button and followed it with a trail of kisses winding down towards her pubic hair. Amelia shivered and let out a soft laugh at the gentle sensation Richard's mouth was imparting to her skin. Unconsciously she shifted her legs apart and braced her feet against the floor to raise herself still further.

Richard sat back on his heels and supported her with a hand beneath each of her buttocks. She parted her legs a little more. Richard's dick, which was still poking out from the front of his trousers, stiffened at the sight which was opening up before him. The deep pink lips of Amelia's sex, like some rare and fragile flower, were swelling and slickening even as he watched. The world around him, the stone circle at whose centre they lay, blurred into the deepest background. All the light in the night sky seemed to be concentrating in Amelia, in her body, her sex.

'Touch me,' she begged him, as her own fingers moved instinctively towards her most vulnerable and sensitive place. Her pelvis was now straining up towards his mouth. 'Touch me, Richard.'

Slowly, reverently, Richard dipped his head to her vagina and began to caress the delicate clitoris which was calling out for his attention in the darkness of the night. First he kissed it, then cautiously he poked out his tongue to touch the most sensitive part of her with one of the most sensitive parts of him. At the moment of contact, there escaped a sigh, long and happy, from Amelia's kiss-worn mouth. Richard smiled to himself and continued with the task that he had longed for the pleasure of undertaking. As he slowly licked at her glassy smooth vulva, his fingers gently clenched her buttocks. Her fingers echoed his, tearing up handfuls of the green summer grass which grew thickly all around them. The gentle breeze that crossed the top of the hill had died down. All he could hear was her breathing, deep and measured, echoing around the ancient stones.

After a while she pushed his head away with her hands and sat up. She reached out one hand and touched his penis, which was still so hard, still straining for her attention. She wrapped her fingers around it and pumped it rhythmically while they kissed again. Richard caught his breath. She sensed that she was perhaps pushing him too far and slowed her careful manipulation of his member down a little, so that he could regain control and avoid ending this precious moment in a fountain all over the grass.

Amelia's free hand tangled in her own pubic hair again, probing the folds that Richard's tongue had left behind. She was thinking about the penis she was holding, about how nicely he could fill her, how much she wanted him to take her now, and the muscles of her vagina contracted in sympathy with her thoughts. She began to lie back down on the ground, slowly, pulling him over her as she did so, still holding his penis, guiding him towards the centre of her body. She drew her knees up and let them fall apart so that she was open to him, completely open. Their mouths never parted, they continued to kiss all the while.

As Richard's tongue penetrated her mouth, she gently swayed her pelvis up to meet his and with the gentlest of pushes on Richard's part, his penis and her vagina were also joined. Amelia wrapped her arms tightly around his body and they pulled together as hard as they could, holding the position, the moment. Just letting their bodies melt into each other, his hand twisting into her soft red hair, her hands around his back, clasping him as if her fingers would break through his skin and flow into his blood.

Then they began to move. So effortlessly in time with one another. Their bodies swaying together and apart again almost soundlessly. Richard held himself up on locked arms and gazed down at the space between them, at his penis moving in and out of Amelia's vagina. The thick rod appearing and disappearing. She watched the graceful curve of her pelvis as it moved up to meet his, the tension in her stomach muscles, and in his stomach muscles. She reached between them to pull his T-shirt up out of the way so that she could see the action better. She held his waist between her hands, enjoying the feeling of his hard flesh flexing beneath her fingers with each thrust.

Richard's face took on a look of intense concentration as he moved to bring her maximum delight. His hair flopped in sweat-soaked strands over his eyes. Amelia's hands roamed ecstatically over his body, on his bare flesh beneath his T-shirt. He was so smooth, so warm, so obviously full of love for her.

'Richard,' she murmured, as a particularly deep thrust touched her G-spot and made the stars from the sky dance for a moment in front of her eyes. He was looking right into those eyes now, his heart pleading through his gaze for her to say something more, something deeper. To say perhaps that she loved him as he loved her? But she was on the point of being lost. Her back was arching up, her throat thrown upwards to the watching sky. Her mouth parted to let forth her breath in pants and sighs as it became increasingly uncontrolled.

'Richard,' she called again as another thrust hit the mark. She gazed up at him through languorously lowered eyelids. On this grass that moved like waves in the breeze, she was like a siren, tempting him, drawing him into his doom. The blue cast that the moon gave her skin made her look as though he was seeing her through water. Water that separated them, that held them still apart even when they were so joined. Her hands slid silently over his skin. One of her bare feet rubbed against his lower leg.

'Kiss me.'

Richard kissed her again. Her lips were cooled by the breeze. He pulled away. She gave a tiny, desperate moan. He recognised the clenching of her beautiful fingers on his buttocks as she tried to force the pace to get faster. He recognised the rising pitch of her sighs. They came faster and faster, until the time between them was negligible and Amelia erupted in one long keening call of bliss.

Richard felt himself lose control at that moment too. His movements, once so smooth, were all wrong, all out of time. They came together and yet apart. Each in a separate world of desire. Feeling different feelings. Thinking different thoughts as their bodies crashed and crushed each other. Semen mixed with sweat.

Richard collapsed onto Amelia's quivering body, his face in the cool, green grass. Her chest heaved. Her breathing deafened him. Her hands had left his body and lay loosely beside her. She had let him go.

Later, they got up and drove back to London. Still jet-lagged, Amelia slept in the car.

Chapter Thirteen

TWO DAYS LATER, it was as if the night in the stone circle had never happened.

Amelia had recorded a demo tape at the studio of a friend of Jerry's. She was doing about two gigs a week now. On Tuesday she was playing at the Lamb and Flag. Richard wished her luck but this time he didn't ask to go along. He would wait until he was invited.

Before she was due to start playing, Amelia joined the promoter of the gig for a drink. He had just popped to the gents, leaving her alone at the bar, when she saw Jamie Nettles stroll in. He had no girl in tow this time but he was looking handsome as ever in a green silk shirt and black jeans. Amelia read the back of a beermat, thinking he hadn't noticed her, but it wasn't long before she heard the clatter of his cowboy boots on the floorboards behind her and a reptilian hand came to rest lightly on her bare white shoulder.

'Amelia,' he said, kissing the back of her long neck. 'You've been avoiding my calls.'

'Jamie,' she trilled falsely. She twisted out of his mouth's reach but decided there was no point in being rude. 'I haven't. I've tried to call you hundreds of times but your phone is just perpetually engaged. You must be a very popular guy.' He seemed happy enough with her answer.

'You look great tonight.'

'Thank you.' Amelia sipped her drink and waited for him to slip into the audience, but he didn't.

'What are you doing after you've played?' Jamie asked suddenly. He shifted slightly from foot to foot. 'Do you fancy going to get something to eat? We could go to that Mexican place again.'

'Thanks for asking, Jamie, but, no, I've got to get home as soon as I finish here tonight.'

'Rubbish, Amelia. Tell you what, I'll give you a lift. I'd really like to talk to you about getting a contract signed – soon. Some kind of development deal.'

'Really?' Amelia bit her lip, remembering what Richard had told her at the weekend. Was Jamie really just lying to her about her chances in the music business to get her into bed? She decided she couldn't risk the chance that he was actually being genuine. 'OK,' she told him. 'But just a quick bite, yeah?'

'Well,' said Amelia as they left the restaurant and headed for Jamie's car. 'Now that we've eaten, I really do need to be getting home. I've got a temping job in the morning,' she lied.

'But we haven't really talked about that deal yet,' Jamie protested. 'Come back to my place for a coffee.'

Amelia turned round in her seat to look him straight in the eye.

'Jamie, is there really a deal at all?'

A flicker of panic crossed his face but then he smiled broadly. 'Would I lie to you?' He reached into the glove compartment of the dashboard and brought out an envelope which he waved before her nose with a flourish. Amelia made a grab for it but he kept it just out of her reach.

'Oh, no. Don't look at it now,' he said. 'I think you really need me to go through this with you.' Jamie was already pulling his car out of the narrow road in the direction of his flat in Camden, the exact opposite direction to Amelia's home.

Amelia sat casually on Jamie's deep sofa, arms crossed, one leg crossed over the knee of the other. She thought her posture made it quite clear that she was in the mood for nothing but business. She was determined to overcome the power of the past events associated with the sofa upon which she now sat. Jamie emerged from the kitchen with two familiar balloon glasses. He had lost only a little of the self-assurance which had so charmed her the first time they met.

'Calvados,' he told her.

'Of course,' she replied. He sat down beside her. Amelia shifted across the seat so that the gap between the cushions would act as a psychological divide. She crossed her legs away from him. 'So, let's talk business.'

'In a minute,' he told her. 'Let's have a drink first. What ever is wrong with you?'

'I suppose you could say that I'm feeling a little "nettled",' she replied. Jamie laughed uneasily.

'*Pourquoi*?' he asked suavely.

'Well, dear Jamie, rumour has it that it isn't exactly my musical talent which keeps you coming back to see me play.'

'I'm sorry?' Jamie feigned ignorance.

Amelia snapped.

'I mean that you're only interested in my body, you creep.'

'Amelia, that's unfair.' Jamie racked his brain for a suitably calming come-back to her accusation. 'You know that I'm interested in your music first and foremost ... But how could any red-blooded male not be interested in the whole package, as it were? You're a beautiful woman, Amelia. I won't deny that I'd still love to see you if you had the talent of a recently deceased flea.'

'And do I?'

'Do you what?'

'Have the talent of a flea?'

'Amelia, you have the talent of the most talented ...' he struggled to find the words. 'Amelia, I struggle to find the words to express quite exactly how very talented you are.'

Her expression lightened a little.

'And I am sure that everyone at Gallagher

Records, from the MD to the receptionist, will feel the same.' He took hold of her hand and was inwardly very pleased when she didn't struggle to wrench it free. Amelia was purring inside. Jamie tickled her inner wrist with one of his fingers. He had read in some psychology book that this kind of subtle physical contact was a sure way to break down someone's defences.

'Show me the contract, Jamie,' Amelia said suddenly. She was the hard-nosed American businesswoman once again.

'Yes, sure.' Jamie popped into his bedroom and reappeared with the envelope he had shown her in the car. He sat back down beside her. She had moved across her psychological divide so that her knee now touched his thigh. She even went so far as to lean upon his shoulder. Jamie shuffled the pieces of paper inside the envelope and brought out page two.

'What about page one?' Amelia asked.

'Oh, that's got nothing interesting on it,' Jamie mumbled. Just your name and address and Gallagher Records' name and address and a load of old codswallop about the law of the land . . .'

Amelia seemed happy enough with his inexpansive explanation and so Jamie started to go through the contract from clause two. By the time he had touched upon the 'outstandingly generous' advance and royalty figures she was silly putty in his hands.

'So you mean you really think I have two albums in me already?' she asked breathlessly.

'At least,' Jamie told her, putting the final sheet back into the envelope. Amelia reached for the manila folder of her desire. 'Hang on,' said Jamie, taking it back from her hurriedly. 'You can't have this just yet. It has to go to the legal department first. I'll tell them that you're happy with all the terms and then they will send you a copy of your very own to sign.'

'Oh, thank you, Jamie, thank you,' Amelia gushed. 'I can't begin to tell you just how grateful I am.'

Jamie smiled. 'I'm sure you can.'

They had another big glass of Calvados to celebrate. The peace treaty of a contract had by now done a Berlin Wall job on the psychological divide and Amelia sprawled happily across Jamie's lap. Her head rested in his crotch and she suddenly didn't mind when she felt the familiar twitch of an awakening hard-on near her ear. He was stroking her hair. She reached up to toy with one of the buttons on his green silk shirt, commented on how nice the little piece of mother-of-pearl was and then proceeded to unfasten it. Jamie bent down to kiss her smiling lips. At last the game was back on.

Minutes later Jamie scooped Amelia up in his arms and carried her straight through to the bedroom. Since her last visit he had bought a new bed. It was made of dark wood, with beautifully sculpted bed knobs at the top and the bottom. It was piled high with pillows, covered in pure white cotton. A dream of a bed with a mattress

172

two feet thick.

'It's lovely,' Amelia murmured. 'Really beautiful.'

'Want to help me break it in?' Jamie asked, pitching her onto its huge, soft marshmallow middle. She fell giggling from his arms and was immediately swallowed by the duvet and pillows which bounced up around her. Jamie stood at the side of the bed, pinched his nose as if he were about to jump into a swimming pool and joined her on the pillows with a dive.

They kicked off their shoes and rolled about like children, ripping off their clothes frantically in a race to get naked and beneath the luxurious covers. Amelia was pleased to see that she had not imagined how gorgeous Jamie's body really was in the light of the Calvados of their first meeting. She ran her fingers excitedly all over him, measuring his smooth brown shoulders, his firm pecs and biceps. She kissed him lightly on each nipple, bringing forth the first of many happy little groans she would hear before they had finished.

Jamie responded in kind. Amelia thrilled to his touch. So knowing, so professional even, she laughed to herself. Her nipples stiffened into little rose-pink cones beneath his fingers. As he bent forward to return the kisses she had given him, Amelia grasped his straw-blond head and hugged it tightly to her chest. She relished the rough feeling of his stubble against her delicate white skin.

'Kiss me, kiss me,' she whispered, pulling his mouth up to meet hers. He had such a sexy way of kissing, of biting her lips and nibbling at their red fullness. He tasted of Calvados and cigarette smoke. He was delicious.

Jamie's hand had already found its way between Amelia's legs. It rocked back and forth against her mound, his fingers just touching her clitoris and slightly tingling labia. As they kissed, Amelia pressed her body down against his hand to increase the sensation. She needed more pressure to satisfy the feeling that was beginning to mount inside her. Her lips were awakening, swelling gradually larger to meet his touch. It was almost as if she could feel herself opening up to him. She put her hand down between their bodies and took hold of his hand, guiding his middle finger into her velvet-lined channel.

Jamie sighed as he felt the soft, warm walls of her vagina close around his knuckle. His dick twitched upwards, longing to replace the finger and be enclosed to the hilt in her delicious wet heat.

'Your pussy feels so gorgeous,' he told her.

'You're so crude,' Amelia couldn't help laughing.

'It's the best description I could find for a girl who is as much of an animal as you are. A vixen. No, a real tiger.' He twisted a fingerful of her fluffy red pubic hair. 'And you're so wet. Wet as a swimming pool. It just makes me want to dive right in.'

'Go on then,' she challenged. She wrapped her fingers around his shaft and used it to pull him towards her. She was straddling his lap now, sitting on his upper thighs with her feet dangling over the edge of the bed. She wrapped her arms around his tanned neck and eased her body upwards so that the tip of his dick was pointing at the entrance to her vagina. Jamie took his hand away so that his glans was actually touching Amelia's labia. She rocked slowly back and forth, undulated across him so that the pinky head dragged over her smooth coral flesh, wet with longing for him. Jamie shivered.

'Dive right in,' she echoed his suggestion.

Jamie took hold of his penis and carefully began to guide it inside her. Amelia shuffled into position, easing herself down inch by inch until she felt Jamie's balls make contact with her bottom. His face and neck were flushing hotly with long anticipated rapture.

Jamie was kneeling on the bed. Amelia drew her knees up and awkwardly arranged herself so that she too was now kneeling and could move herself up and down Jamie's slippery shaft by simply bending and then straightening her knees. Her arms were still wrapped around his neck. She looked deep into his eyes. They were black with arousal. She wondered if hers looked the same. His lower lip trembled delicately as she oozed up and down.

'Stay still,' she told him when the tempo began to build and he tried to alter the pace by making movements of his own. With each downward thrust, she tightened her vaginal muscles around him as hard as she could. He seemed to be enjoying it, each squeeze eliciting a shuddering sigh, but suddenly, he grasped her around the waist and forcibly rolled her over so that she was firmly on the bottom.

'Jamie!' Amelia gasped, thrilled by his unexpected decision to take charge. Her legs shook as he began to power into her from this new position. She tried to lift her body up to meet his but he was already going much too hard, too fast. Then Jamie slid his hands beneath her buttocks to raise her slender hips up so that he could go even deeper still.

'Ow,' Amelia cried as Jamie's marble-hard shaft touched the front wall of her vagina and sent through her a peculiarly pleasurable shock.

'Did that hurt?' he asked with a grunt which was almost concerned as he continued to grind away.

'Oh, God, no,' she told him. 'Carry on, carry on.' She helped him by grasping his buttocks and moving them herself. She wanted to open up more and more and more, to let him so far inside her that he would almost split her in half. As she closed her eyes, a picture of the man in Las Vegas suddenly flashed across the movie screen of her mind. The dangerous pleasure she had felt at being totally at the mercy of a strange but attractive man. Of the terrible instant animal passion that accompanies lust rather than love.

Amelia was calling out as she had never done before. She was helpless now. Totally at the mercy of the power of her desire. She felt that she couldn't move at all and yet her whole being was buzzing, writhing inside.

Jamie grasped one of Amelia's thighs and pulled her tingling leg up towards her chest. He powered into her at an angle now. She felt open, open, open. Quaking, she tried in vain to touch her own sex, her fingers getting caught in the crush of his pelvis on hers. She was so wet. The juice of her desire for him was already running down the inside of her trembling thigh. It was shiny and clear and oh-so sticky. Her arousal was reaching its maximum. Or maybe she was about to go one further than she ever had before.

'Jamie, Jamie, stop, stop, stop!' she squealed, though the laughter in her voice and the insistence of her hands driving his buttocks told him that that was not what she actually meant this time. She felt as though every drop of blood in her body was rushing to her vagina now. Her head was light, giddy, dizzy. Bright flashes of every colour swam before her eyes.

Jamie too felt his entire body harden towards his goal. He was seconds away now. His balls ached to be free of their load. To shoot hot jets of come deep inside her.

Jamie's body reared up and twisted away from her as he began to climax violently. His face contorted. His teeth were bared, gritted together. Sperm thundered through his penis to explode into Amelia's body. Beneath him she thrashed. Her own pleasure was breaking her in two . . . Her pelvis rose automatically to meet his downward thrusts. She wrapped her legs around his, holding them together, reeling him in.

'My God!' Jamie shouted suddenly as the last of his come left him with a shudder. Amelia pressed herself against him. Her own body calming down now. The violent spasms of her orgasm becoming a vibration that was slowing to a distant and gentle hum.

Amelia clutched Jamie's exhausted body to her own. His back was slick and wet with sweat. She drew her fingers across it, stroking him until she knew he had fallen asleep.

After an hour or so of lying beside him, eyes open and wide awake, Amelia left Jamie snoring and crept out of the bedroom. Like a thief she tiptoed back into the sitting-room where the brown envelope containing the contract still lay upon the couch. She pulled it out carefully, determined to get one more look at the terms before Jamie had her own copy sent on.

Now that it was finally in her hands, she flicked over the first page, the page which Jamie had kept tucked out of the way while he showed her the important clauses. The first page of the contract which held nothing but the boring information like names and addresses and the law of the land. Names and addresses were there all right, but not one of them was hers!

In fact, the recording contract which Jamie had been showing her was not hers at all. It was made out to another artist entirely. To add insult to injury it was in the name of one of the heavy metal acts she had been supporting on the night she and Jamie first met. The words of the contract swam before Amelia's confused eyes until she shredded the flimsy pages in fury and disbelief. She had played again with Jamie Nettles and once again, she'd been stung.

Chapter Fourteen

'YOU BASTARD, JAMIE Nettles, you utter, utter bastard,' Amelia hissed at the closed door of the bedroom where he lay, oblivious to her hate. 'You are going to pay for this.'

Amelia arranged the tiny pieces of the shredded contract into a neat little pyramid while she formulated some horrifying plan for revenge. She looked around the stark designer sitting-room for inspiration. Jamie's personally engraved Zippo lighter lay with his car keys on the coffee table. Amelia glanced back at the little bonfire she had already made on the floor and sighed. Perhaps she should set fire to his beautiful flat, she thought. His expensive pale wooden floor-boards wouldn't look quite so good with a hole burnt in the middle of them . . .

'No, don't be stupid,' she chastised herself quickly. Jamie Nettles wasn't worth ending up in jail for . . . Murder and arson were right out of the question. Anyway, what this particular arsehole needed was a taste a little closer to his own brand of medicine. Amelia picked up a few pieces of the contract and let them flutter through her fingers. She chewed her lip ruminatively as she racked her brains for the perfect scenario. What Jamie Nettles needed was something which would hurt him far more deeply than physical pain.

'Humiliation,' she finally muttered. Yes, that was the word she was looking for. Humiliation.

As silently as she had left the bedroom, Amelia crept back into it and reinstalled herself at Jamie's side in the plush new bed. He was still snoring, and hadn't moved an inch so she figured he had no idea of her recent discovery. Amelia propped herself up on the pillows and surveyed the bedroom for suitable instruments of torture. As an A & R man in the music industry, constantly going to sweaty gigs to hunt out new talent, Jamie Nettles rarely had the need for a tie, but he had belts. Six or seven of them. Black and brown. Soft, smooth leather with elaborate silver buckles. Amelia could see them now, hanging up neatly in his partially open mirrored wardrobe. They would be perfect.

Amelia slid out of the bed and crept to the cupboard. Yes. The belts were just what she had in her furious mind. She picked out four and felt their satisfactory weight in her hands. How unfortunate for Jamie that he had just bought himself such an obliging new bed. She sincerely hoped that the silver buckles wouldn't leave any nasty notches in his lovingly varnished bed-posts.

'Jamie,' she whispered over his slumbering body. 'Jamie, Jamie.' Each time she spoke his name just a little louder than before. But she got no response from the body on the bed. He was out cold. Dead to the world. No way was this dream-boy waking up.

'Good.'

He was sleeping on his front. Amelia carefully took hold of his right wrist and stretched out his arm so that it reached to the corner of the bed. She fastened it to the bed-post with a belt. Jamie stirred slightly and gave a quiet moan, but he didn't wake. Amelia did the same with his other limbs until he was fastened into position, face down. Moments later, Amelia had pulled off all the sheets and his pert, firm buttocks were bared to the ceiling, but still Jamie was lost in his dreams.

Now for the pièce de résistance, Amelia grinned. In the glass vase that stood on Jamie's bedside cabinet was a bunch of long-stemmed white carnations. Amelia selected the biggest and most beautiful bloom for her purposes, but knew that she would have to complete the rest of her arrangements before she could risk placing that where it deserved to go.

Back in the sitting-room, on the coffee table next to his keys and his Zippo, Jamie's personal organiser sat quietly holding his secrets between its leather covers. Amelia knew the number she was looking for, and it was scribbled on the very first page. Jamie's office. She dialled it purpose-fully and then waited for his voice-mail box to

182

kick in. When it did, she covered the receiver with her hand and prayed that he had a secretary who would check his messages when morning came and Jamie didn't turn up for work.

'Er . . . I'm not well, can somebody please come and collect my papers from me at home,' Amelia muttered in a suitably deep voice. She hoped that they would think any strangeness in it was due to a sore throat.

Now for the flower.

'Oh, Jamie, you're such a heavy sleeper,' Amelia sighed as she pushed the delicate stem of the crisp white bloom gently between the twin brown orbs of his bum. He didn't budge an inch. The flower stood up proudly like a tree growing between two hills. Amelia stood back and admired her handiwork. He really did have an incredible body. It was a shame he had turned out to be such a dickhead. It was also a shame, thought Amelia, that she didn't have a nettle instead of a carnation, but she was sure that, after an hour or so, the stem of that flower would be irritating enough for the poor, dear, prostrate love.

Amelia shrugged on her discarded clothes and left the hapless Jamie to await his fate. Sooner or later, someone somewhere would miss him even if the office didn't bother to send anyone to collect his papers. Perhaps that skinny girl he hung around with had a set of keys to the flat. It didn't really matter because whatever happened, Amelia felt sure that Jamie Nettles would never get the better of this girl again.

Chapter Fifteen

RICHARD WAS STILL sitting up, watching an Open University programme about physics, when Amelia got back home. That she was not in a happy mood was evident long before she opened her mouth to tell him about it. First there was the slam of the taxi door, then the slam of the front door, then the slam of her bag on the kitchen table . . .

'You were right,' she wailed as she marched into the sitting-room. 'Jamie Nettles is a total jerk!'

'There, there.' Richard took her in his arms and patted her consolingly. Whatever Jamie Nettles had done, he had just made Richard's day. 'What did he do this time to make you so furious?'

Amelia poured out the story about the contract . . . and the carnation. Richard winced and poured out some tea.

'So, do you think someone from the office will bother to go round to Jamie's house?' Amelia asked.

'I'll make sure of it,' said Richard. All of a sudden he felt that the next morning couldn't come quickly enough.

'It's late,' he said after a while. 'I'm going to turn in.'

Amelia looked at him desperately. She didn't want to be on her own. Not right now. 'Can't you stay up just a tiny bit longer?' she asked. 'I really feel like talking tonight.'

Richard was already standing up to leave. He surveyed Amelia's delicate frame curled up into a defensive ball on the sofa, her bare feet covered by her long flowing skirt. She pushed her soft red hair back with her hands and he saw that, even after the laugh they had shared about Jamie's misfortune, her green-blue eyes were bright with tears.

'OK. But I'll need some coffee,' Richard told her.

'Your wish is my command,' Amelia trilled, jumping up to run to the kitchen.

Richard sank back down into his chair with a groan. He glanced at his watch and sighed when he saw that it was almost four in the morning. Why was he bothering? He didn't want to know about the ways in which so many other men were making Amelia's life a misery when he was sure that, given the chance, he could be the one to really turn her luck around.

She must enjoy being treated badly, Richard reasoned.

Just at that moment, Amelia emerged from the

kitchen with two steaming mugs of coffee.

'Do you think I bring guys like Jamie Nettles upon myself?' she asked.

What a question! Richard bit back the temptation to say the thought had crossed his mind. Instead he gritted his teeth and assured her that guys like Jamie Nettles brought themselves upon most attractive single girls.

'I know that I could have avoided tonight in some ways, though . . . I really didn't intend to end up in bed with him but . . . Oh, I don't know, I suppose I just like sex too much. A guy like Jamie just has to sit there looking gorgeous and no matter how often I tell myself that I will hate him and me in the morning, I have to go for it . . . I have to get him into bed . . . I think I must have the highest sex drive of anybody I know,' she continued, blissfully ignorant to any pain her musings might be causing. 'And sometimes it's even better to go to bed with someone you know doesn't really give a shit . . .'

Richard looked at her sadly. He wondered if she really thought that, or whether her words were just the bravado of someone who felt she had never really been loved.

'Do you really believe that?' he asked.

'Yeah, I do,' she said blithely. 'It's much more passionate, more animal, when you can have the sex without the hassle of emotional bonds. Love can keep you warm at night but only lust can make you burn.'

'That's just sad, Amelia,' Richard told her

186

wearily. 'And you know that it's not even true. If it was, you wouldn't have bothered to take out your revenge on Jamie, you would have said 'Thanks very much' when you left in the morning – and you certainly wouldn't be bothered that Jerry isn't coming home from the States yet. Don't you love him?'

'Of course.'

'And he's great in bed?'

'Yes.'

'Better than me?'

'I don't want to answer that, Richard. Why ask me that?' Amelia said defensively.

'I just wondered whether you can really tell the difference between sex with love and sex with lust.'

Amelia looked away from Richard and drained her coffee mug.

The conversation had died between them now. Richard made to get up again.

'Are you angry with me?' Amelia asked.

'I just don't like to see you being used, Amelia,' Richard told her. 'Nobody likes to be used.' He began to walk towards the stairs. He heard Amelia sniff loudly behind him. It was the herald of another outburst of tears. Just what he needed at four in the morning. But this time, Richard decided, he wasn't going to be her bloody shoulder to cry on. Every time he made things better for her she would run off and ruin them with someone else the very next day. But the strangled little sobs grew more and more insistent until Richard could bear no more and, having just reached the top of the stairs, he ran all the way back down them again.

'Oh, don't cry, Amelia,' he cooed, taking her in his arms again and smoothing back her beautiful hair in his familiar way. 'I didn't mean to upset you.'

'Oh, Richard,' Amelia wailed. 'Can I stay in your room tonight? I'm just not going to be able to sleep on my own.'

'Amelia, no,' he insisted. 'No. I'll be just next door if you need me.'

'I need you now.'

'No, you don't.'

Richard struggled to keep his resolve. He managed, just, and persuaded her to sleep in her own room after all. But ten minutes of hearing her pathetic sobs and sniffs through the thin wall later, he found himself wandering in there to be with her.

'Oh, I'm sorry,' she continued to sniff. Her eyes were bright red around the rims from crying. Richard sat on the edge of the bed beside her and administered comforting banalities until he was forced by the chilliness of the room to get in under the covers. At once, Amelia's slender arms wrapped themselves around him like the tentacles of an octopus. Richard felt his heart beat increase its speed. Something sexual stirred deep inside him. It mustn't happen though, he told himself. He must not let it happen. He would be just as bad as Jamie Nettles if he let her seduce him now.

Amelia's fingers played hesitantly with the hair on his chest. He put a comforting arm around her shoulders and tried to resist becoming any more familiar than that.

'Don't,' he said when her fingers crept towards his nipple.

'Why not?' she asked. But before he had time to explain, she had silenced his protestations with a kiss.

Richard tried not to respond to her lips but it was growing increasingly impossible. When she showed no sign of giving up on him, he reluctantly folded his arms right around her and yielded to the insistence of her kiss.

'We shouldn't be doing this,' he protested when they came up for air. 'You don't really want to do this with me. You're just confused because of Jerry and Jamie Nettles.'

'Oh shut up, Richard,' Amelia said suddenly. 'Just kiss me now and let me hate you in the morning.'

She laughed at her own little joke. Richard was strangely comforted by it. And he supposed that it was she who had begged him to keep her company. He wasn't really using her if she wanted this. But, hang on, he told himself, wasn't it he who was being used?

'What if I don't want to do this?' he began. But it was too late. Amelia had her hand on the rapidly bulging front of his shorts. He had been betrayed by his body yet again. Amelia massaged him expertly so that any protest he tried to make from that moment on came out as a cross between a groan and an ecstatic sigh.

'Oh god,' he groaned as he felt himself finally going under his desire for the girl in the bed beside him. Amelia had disappeared beneath the sheets now and he could only anticipate the hot lick of her tongue on the end of his faithless knob.

'Oh shit,' Richard moaned as Amelia wriggled his dick free of his shorts and began to suck the sensitive tip. She pulled back the tightly fitting foreskin and flicked at his bared glans with her tongue. It was salty with pre-come, and smooth as a dick fashioned in molten glass.

'Amelia,' he wailed as she took his balls in one hand and gently tickled them with the long fingernails of the other. She had won him over completely now. His mind had been vanquished by the will of the twitching balls in her palm. His dick stiffened until it could have held the blankets up on its own. Richard felt the semen beginning to build within him, crowding towards the head of his dick, begging to be allowed to make its sticky escape.

'Oh no, please.' If she didn't move very quickly, he was going to have to come in her mouth.

Amelia made no effort to move away, though the jerky movements of Richard's dick to and fro inside the cavern of her mouth told her that a climax was not too far off. She continued to lick at him frantically, sucking the purple tip between her lip-covered teeth. But her fingers were still massaging his balls, pulling them slightly down-wards whenever she heard the pre-climactic groan, to prolong the agonising joy just a little longer.

Richard's hands were beneath the covers now, grasping at her hair, moving her head up and down, faster and faster. Almost too fast. His fingers flexed with a sudden spasm. Amelia sucked at him extra hard.

'Oh, no. I'm nearly there.'

He was there.

Amelia sucked avidly as the first of the hot semen began to spurt into her waiting mouth. She swallowed as he spurted, feeling the warm liquid oozing down the back of her throat and almost wishing that she had given him the chance to explode somewhere else. But for now, all she could do was make sure that she didn't spill a drop.

The last spasm of Richard's unwanted orgasm racked his body and left him panting on the pillows. He laid a hand on his heart, feeling it beat faster and harder than it had done after any marathon. Amelia emerged from beneath the covers, sweating with the heat of being under two blankets and wiping her sticky mouth on the back of her hand. Richard wasn't the only one who had been exerting himself. Amelia flopped onto half the pillow where Richard's head lay and gazed at his handsome, chiselled profile as he lay trying to catch his fleeting breath.

'Don't you ever, ever do that again,' said Richard.

'That I just can't promise,' said Amelia.

The morning sun poured in through the thin yellow curtains of Amelia's room and woke Richard up. For a moment, he wasn't sure where he was. Then he remembered. He gazed lovingly at the sleeping figure beside him. Her nose was whistling slightly as she breathed in and out. So, in spite of all his good intentions they had gone and done it again. How long did he have before the bubble burst this time?

The postman answered that one.

Richard trundled down the stairs to pick up the post which had been dropped through the front door. The gas bill, a Reader's Digest circular and a little package for Amelia. Jerry's personal assistant was sending her the spare keys to his flat. Jerry wouldn't be home for a while but he wanted her to move back in anyway. Though she hid it quite well, Richard knew that Amelia was pleased. The one condition was that she didn't bring back the cat.

Amelia moved her things back into Jerry's flat that very weekend.

Richard got to keep Eliza.

Chapter Sixteen

AMELIA LET HERSELF into Jerry's echoing flat and locked the door behind her. The answer-machine's alert button was flashing. She listened to the messages. Jerry's mother, three times. Jerry himself, calling to say that he was going to be delayed for just another day or so. What a surprise.

Amelia draped her coat across the back of a chair and wandered into the kitchen. She mixed herself a large gin and tonic, but found that there was no ice. Cursing, she stuck the drink in the freezer compartment to cool it down a little more. She leant against the work surface. Better get myself something to eat, I suppose, she thought. She opened a couple of barren cupboards. There was no point in cooking anything elaborate for one. A bag of cheese and onion crisps nestled between two dusty packets of dried pasta in sauce. Crisps? Pasta? She would eat the crisps while she was cooking the pasta.

The phone rang, but the caller hung up before Amelia could get across the long sitting-room to answer it. Somehow, the sudden and brief ringing of the phone made the silence seem all the more oppressive. Spooky. Amelia didn't really like being in the flat by herself any more, though she had often spent time alone there before her flight to Kentish Town. It would be better when Jerry came back, she reassured herself. She just needed company.

Jerry had a television in the kitchen. He had televisions all over the place. He subscribed to satellite and cable, because he hated to think that he might be missing something new and exciting while he was watching BBC2. Amelia flicked on the set on the breakfast bar for the comfort of the background noise while she cooked.

'And coming up later on "The Next Big Thing",' announced the wide-mouthed girl on MTV, 'an exclusive, and live, interview with London band The Dolphins who have been recording their second album here in Los Angeles. See them right after the break.'

Amelia swivelled round from the hob to look at the little screen. 'The Dolphins?' Wasn't that the name of the band Jerry was working with? Well, if he wasn't going to be coming home for a while, she could at least find out what he had been up to in Los Angeles since she left. See if he'd got this 'next-big-thing' of his playing in tune, at least. Jerry would be pleased to know that she was taking an interest in one of his projects.

The adverts flashed and flickered in a stream of mind-assaulting sound-bites. It seemed as if they were never going to end. Amelia turned the hob down to a simmering heat and opened the strongly flavoured crisps. No doubt there would be another ten minutes or so of waffle from the babe in the glasses again before they got around to the promised clip anyway.

The programme restarted. This time the presenter was pictured standing by a bar in a dingy club. Faux cobwebs hung from marble-painted pillars which were lit by purple and green coloured bulbs. The wrought iron stools were upholstered in blood red velvet.

'I'm here in the bar of The Batcave in Santa Monica, where I'm going to be joining British band The Dolphins who are in Los Angeles to record their second album . . .'

'Yeah, yeah. Get on with it,' Amelia muttered.

'The Dolphins were last here in 1992, when they toured with their multi-million-selling album "Wide Sargasso Sea". This latest album has been three years in the making but they think they're almost there. Here's how you might remember them . . .'

The programme cut to a clip from an old video. The impossibly handsome lead singer stared mournfully out over a misty bay, where two dolphins, strangely enough, turned gracefully in the air before splashing back into the grey-blue water. The picture of freedom. Amelia guessed that the creatures were probably on loan from a theme park.

Two choruses later, they were back in The Batcave. Now the presenter was slinking over to a candle-lit table. Amelia recognised the singer sitting on the right. There were four other band members at the table and two more guys who were in shadow for the moment. The presenter rattled through some names which all sounded as if they had been made up.

'And Jerry Anson,' she added finally, 'who flew all the way over from England to finish producing this album at the eleventh hour when Michael Hammerstein unexpectedly pulled out of the project after artistic differences . . .'

The camera panned to Jerry's familiar face, a cigar at the corner of his mouth. He waved his hand lazily for the audience before the presenter got back to interviewing the more aesthetically-pleasing members of the bunch.

Amelia stuck with the pretentious drivel about finding oneself as an artist for ten minutes. The camera was fixed in close-up on the singer or the drummer's face for most of that time. Then they went to another video, promising to go back to The Batcave before the show was over. Amelia turned her attention back to the pasta which was already fast congealing in the bottom of the pan. She got a fork and picked at it. Not good, but not entirely inedible. An advert for something altogether more appetising filled the screen until, as promised, they were back at The Batcave.

'Hi, I'm Samantha Dean reporting for "Next Big Thing" from Santa Monica's Batcave. With me are The Dolphins . . .'

The singer was sitting beside Samantha at the bar now, nursing a tall pink drink with a lot of silly cocktail accessories sticking out of the top of it. Some people were dancing in the background and it was to these revellers that Amelia's eye was drawn.

Instantly Amelia recognised the spasmodically jerking figure that was Jerry. He had probably learned a strange variation on a jitterbug back in the Seventies when he might have cut a slightly more svelte figure on the dance-floor. Amelia allowed herself a little chuckle. But then she thought she saw the undulations of someone else she recognised. Dancing next to Jerry. The camera irritatingly switched back to Samantha before her suspicions could be confirmed.

Amelia waited, her fork hovering in mid-air between the pan and her mouth while she concentrated on the screen. Back to the dancers. Jerry was obscured now, obscured by the tall, slim body of a young woman that had been wrapped around Amelia's own body just a couple of weeks before. The girl had her arms about Jerry's neck. She was grinding her pelvis against his generous waistline. She was even kissing the shiny top of his head.

Suddenly, it was all becoming horribly clear. The Batcave in Santa Monica. The man in the music business with the funny accent. His name wasn't Jeffrey as Karis had misheard, but Jerry. Karis had met the man of her dreams and Amelia was about to be plunged into a nightmare.

'Oh no.' Amelia killed the television immediately and put the pan she was holding down very slowly in the sink. 'It can't be true. Not again. Not Karis.'

She looked desperately at her watch. It was four in the morning. It would be just eight in the evening in LA. Amelia had at least another eight hours ahead of her before Karis would be at home and contactable, and that was assuming the unlikely event that she went back to her own home at all.

'What can I do?' Amelia moaned to herself. She paced the sitting-room. She didn't even have Eliza to hug.

Amelia's red address book lay by the phone. She started at the beginning of the alphabet and worked on through. The friends that mattered, she remembered her mother once saying, were the ones you could call up at four o'clock in the morning. She had reached the Ms before she realised that the only friends she had that really mattered were Karis and a certain boy in Kentish Town. And how could she call either of those two that night?

Chapter Seventeen

AT FIRST, RICHARD thought that the ringing of the telephone was just part of his dream. After the fifteenth ring, however, he was beginning to wake up and realised that the insistent tone was very much part of his reality.

It was probably someone calling from America for Amelia, he thought irritably as he pulled on his dressing gown and stumbled down the stairs. Hadn't she let her friends know that she had moved back into Jerry's flat again? As he grunted 'hello' into the receiver, the very last thing Richard expected was for the person on the other end of the line to be Amelia herself.

'Richard, it's me,' she sobbed. 'I need to come home.'

Half an hour later, Amelia was restarting her new life in Kentish Town. Jerry's trusty Shogun was parked on the pavement outside Richard's house again and he was struggling in with arms full of clothes and natural linen lampshades while Amelia made the tea.

'She's my best friend, Richard,' Amelia was wailing. 'And she's stolen my boyfriend. Again.'

'But it seems as though she doesn't know that she's doing anything to hurt you,' Richard explained patiently. 'After all, she doesn't know that her "Jeffrey" is your Jerry.'

'Yes, but he does.'

After listening to the saga for a fifth time and offering a new permutation of the same advice, Richard made his excuses and went to bed. He had to go into work the next morning, even though it was the weekend, to sort out some messy figures for a board meeting. He'd talk to her when he got back. Amelia sat up for just a little longer before she retired to her old room.

Amelia made up her bed and slipped reluctantly between the cool covers. She lay with her arms folded on the outside of the sheets and gazed up at the familiar crack in the ceiling. Her mind was racing, but she was surprised to find that she didn't feel so bad any more, just a little sad that she had cocked up once more in her choice of Mr Wonderful. She would survive all this shit. She had lived without Jerry before and she would do it again. She was young, she was talented, she had friends . . .

Amelia rolled over in bed so that she faced the wall which parted Richard's bedroom from her own. She thought she could hear him snoring. She wished that she could sleep. She could sleep much more easily if she had someone to cuddle up to. Silently, she got out of bed and crept across the landing to Richard's door. It was ajar, and she pushed it open without a squeak. When the shaft of light from the landing fell across Richard's bed, Amelia's gaze met with Richard's wide open eyes.

'I couldn't sleep,' she told him.

'Neither could I.'

'Can I come in?' she asked.

'I was hoping you would say that,' said Richard.

He lifted up the side of his duvet and let Amelia curl beneath it. Without any of the previous awkwardness between them, she snuggled in to his side and rested her head on his comfortable shoulder. He stroked her hair carefully, aware that this might be just another port in a storm for her. He would wait for her to make the first move.

Amelia lay with her head on Richard's shoulder and said nothing. Her hand rested lightly on his T-shirt-covered chest. She could feel the hair which covered it through the thin cotton. Gradually she began to move her hand, tracing out the old T-shirt's silly cartoon motif with her fingers. Richard closed his eyes and gave a heavy sigh.

'What's up?' Amelia asked.

'Oh, nothing,' Richard said.

Amelia sat up so that she could look him in the eye.

'I'm afraid I don't believe that. Do you want me to go back to my room?' she asked. She looked at him more seriously than he had ever seen her look before. 'I know what you must be thinking. That I only come back to you when everything goes wrong . . .'

'It had crossed my mind, yes.'

'Well, I must come back to you for a reason.'

Richard could hear his heart beating in his ears. But Amelia wasn't about to expand upon her explanation. Instead, she took his head in her hands and drew his mouth to her lips. This was a logic he just couldn't resist.

Forgetting all the arguments he had had with himself since Amelia had left him on his own again to go back to Jerry, Richard wrapped his arms around her in an all-forgiving and all-permitting embrace. He kissed her hungrily, like someone who thought he had already had his last chance. His tongue eagerly probed the warm interior of her sweet-tasting mouth.

Soon he felt Amelia's fingers creeping to the bottom of his T-shirt. In an instant she had it over his head and off without ever seeming to take her mouth from his lips. It was chilly in the room and Richard quickly pulled Amelia's warm body back to cover his. They fell backwards, still kissing, onto the soft pillows, their arms and legs tangled together in a lover's knot.

Eager to feel Richard's bare skin against hers, Amelia decided that she would undress herself too. She sat up astride his legs and seductively slipped one satin shoe-string strap down over her white shoulder. Then the other. The slippery red material of the delicate slip glided down her body until her breasts were completely naked. Her bare chest was heaving rapidly with the excitement. Richard sat up too to share another kiss, but Amelia suddenly jumped off the bed and stood beside it for a second, letting the nightdress slither down over her slim hips and onto the floor before she jumped back beneath the duvet.

'Oh, you're . . .' Richard searched for a compliment that would do justice to the beautiful body before him.

Amelia's hair was fanned out like a lacy shawl across her shoulders. Her long heavy fringe hid her eyes in shadow so that from time to time they glinted like gem stones discovered in the darkness. She was sitting astride him again, her hands on his waist while he reached out to touch her perfect breasts. But there was something different about her this time. It was a few moments before he realised that something was missing.

The pendant of amber, the precious pendant that Jerry had given her, was gone.

'Your pendant,' he began in a whisper.

'I don't wear that any more,' she confirmed. 'It's gone.' And in those simple words she put the seal on the past and let Richard see that she was finally free enough to build something new . . . something new with him.

'It's really over between me and Jerry this time,'

Amelia continued in a small voice. 'I never really settled at his flat again. It felt as if something was missing. As if I had left something behind when I moved from here . . . and it wasn't just my cat . . .'

Richard felt his stomach grow light and his head turn giddy.

'I missed you,' Amelia whispered. 'When I wanted to share something happy or sad, the person I wanted to share it with was you. The person I was missing all this time was you.'

The words stuck in Richard's throat and he was surprised to feel the tickly prickle of tears behind his eyes.

'Do you mean that?' he asked her.

She just nodded and kissed him. Her hands stroked his stubbly cheek with a tenderness that had been missing from their love-making until this moment. Her kisses fluttered over him, her lips grazing his nose, eyelids and chin.

'I want you so much,' she murmured. Richard couldn't find the breath to agree.

He clasped her slender body to his, big hands moulded around her delicate shoulder blades. The silky smooth feeling of her skin beneath his fingers delighted him all the more now that he felt there was something more behind her advances than pure lust.

Richard slid his hands around to the front of her body until they found her gently rounded breasts with their perfect pink nipples. First he cupped the full orbs, one in each palm, then he rolled each tiny nipple bud between his fingers.

They stiffened quickly into reddening cones. The skin on her breast-bone was glowing with her arousal.

'Richard,' she said, whispering his name like a magic word that would open his heart up to her. He looked deep into her eyes, into the blackness of her pupils. Her cheeks were burning with desire, her lips swollen and red.

Amelia's eyes flickered over his face too, taking in the gorgeous precision of his stubble-enhanced jaw. How had she not noticed his Latin beauty before? The plastic blond perfection of Jamie Nettles and the other cowboys who had passed through her life faded from her thoughts now. Richard was an oil-painting to their pencil sketches. Something other than lust emanated from him, filled the mind behind his adoring eyes. She ran her fingers through his thick dark curls.

Richard gathered up her body and laid her carefully down on the pillows. He moved until he was on top of her, protecting her from his weight with his arms. They kissed. Amelia ran her hands down his torso until they came to rest on either side of his waist. His body was so warm to the touch now that she arched her own body up to meet him, to feel her breasts against his hot, firm chest.

Amelia was already naked. Her fingers slid a little further down Richard's body until she found the waistband of his boxer shorts. The very same Mickey Mouse boxer shorts he had been wearing when she first seduced him in a fit of anger at Jerry, her ex. She made a mental note to get him something a little more suitable to the lover he was as her fingers slipped beneath the elastic and she tugged the shorts off over his bum.

Richard's dick had been hardening almost since the second she climbed into the bed beside him. When the boxer shorts were finally out of the way, it swung up between their bodies, eager for her touch. Amelia obliged quickly, her fingers expertly teasing Richard to the point where he could not wait a moment longer to have her.

Amelia's legs were already parted around his. Richard reached down to place his hand between her thighs. She sighed delightedly as his fingers gently pushed their way through her pubic hair and began to ease her hotly swollen lips apart. Amelia's pelvis rose up to meet him automatically so that her clitoris was against the heel of Richard's hand.

'That's it,' she breathed. 'Rub me there, rub me harder.'

Richard moved his fingers with tiny circular movements over the little bud that contained so much potential for pleasure. Beneath his slowly rotating hand, Amelia's body rose and fell, fluttering with the racing of her heart. She was sighing and groaning, whispering his name. Richard moved his hand from her clitoris to part her labia once more and entered the moist channel of her vagina which was aching for his attention.

She was wet, so wet. Richard entered her with only one finger at first, but soon two fingers were slipping quickly in and out of her body. Moving easily through the shiny juices of her arousal, his fingers brought her closer to the sensation she was looking for. Amelia ground her silky mound upwards against his hand, pushed against him so that, when he penetrated her, he touched the front wall of her vagina, the G-spot, sending hundreds of paralysing shivers from her womb to the farthest reaches of her body.

'Oh, god . . .' Amelia took hold of Richard's wrist as if she was going to move his hand herself. She was still holding on to his dick, furiously pumping the foreskin back and forth until she heard him catch his breath and knew that they ought to stop before it got too late.

'Make love to me,' she begged him now, dragging his penis nearer and nearer to the entrance of her trembling sex. 'I need to feel you inside me. I want to feel like you're part of me.'

Richard removed his fingers from the warm, wet vagina and allowed himself to be drawn towards her. He drew in his breath sharply as the sensitive bare glans of his penis made first contact with the wetness of her pouting labia. She was parting them with her fingers for him, clearing the way.

'Amelia,' Richard breathed as just a gentle nudge on his part let him push his way inside.

The soft velvety walls of her vagina yielded to and then closed around his shaft like a tailored glove of flesh and blood. They were joined together perfectly, made to lie like this. Amelia's mouth rounded to the feeling of exquisite pleasure, then her lips stretched out again into a beatific smile. Her vagina gently throbbed around Richard's penis, welcoming him in, welcoming him inside.

'Move slowly,' she pleaded, knowing that it would take all his will-power to prolong this instant of joy. Their bodies began to move, together and apart. Together and apart, like two halves of the same body. Richard closed his eyes tightly and cut out the world around them. He was tuned in to Amelia's body and Amelia's body alone. He was relishing the warm wetness of her vagina. The satisfying slapping sound as their bodies made contact. Wet skin upon wet skin. The deliciously slippery feel of arousal and sweat.

Amelia focused on the face above hers. Transfigured by love and desire. The smell of their bodies. Musky. Hot. The delicate scent of perfume rising up from her own heated breast. The tantalisingly soft touch of Richard's hair as his head dropped down and dark brown strands stroked her skin.

'Faster now, faster.'

Richard slipped his hands beneath her lithe hips and raised her pelvis up to him. Amelia placed her own hands firmly on his buttocks. Driving him. Guiding him. Holding him still for a second where the penetration was deepest. Their bodies glided apart, accompanied by a symphony of tiny sounds. Wet skin, soft sighs, the whispering of special names.

Richard was there. He collapsed heavily upon her, crushing her breasts beneath his chest. His pelvis continued to rock upon hers. Faster and faster and harder and harder. Amelia moved as much as she could to be with him, to make sure that this was a moment they spent together in every sense of the word.

The muscles down the side of Richard's neck tensed as he reared above her. His pelvis was locked against hers. His penis deep inside her. He was nudging at the entrance to her very womb as his dick began to spurt.

Amelia shuddered as the first sticky bullets of sperm hit their target. Her legs shook uncontrollably as she tensed them against Richard's waist, clamping him to her. Inside, the walls of her vagina trembled with the beginnings of her own orgasm. A low tremor which began in the deepest part of her, tiny spasms of desire spreading out to touch Richard as he powered into her a final time.

'Oh Richard,' she screamed as the stars danced before her eyes once more. Her head was filled simultaneously with a lightness and a blackness which threatened to take her out of this world. She clutched at his muscle-bound back with her hands, dug in her nails. She needed to hold on, hold on to him until the terrible delight which was wracking her body began to subside. Finally she felt she knew why the French call this 'the little death'.

Afterwards, they lay together, their limbs still entangled, their ragged breathing almost perfectly in time. Then, Richard slowly drew himself away from her and knelt with his feet beneath him on the bed.

'Are you OK?' he asked her. She looked as though she would never get her breath back.

'Very OK,' said Amelia.

Chapter Eighteen

'SO YOU'RE STAYING?' asked Richard the next morning as they lay side by side in his double bed.

Amelia nodded.

'If that's OK with you,' she added, knowing that it was, of course.

'And what will you do with yourself now that Jerry is out of the picture and Jamie Nettles' promises of a contract came to nothing? Are you still going to try to get into the music scene?'

'I don't need either of them. I can make new contacts. I'll carry on writing my songs and one day, I will get a deal.' She looked truly optimistic.

Richard smiled. 'I know you will, too.' He rolled over in the bed and gave her a happy hug. 'By the way, some guy has been phoning you here. Very posh accent. Says his name is Henry Du Pre. Is he anyone I should be jealous of?'

A broad smile spread across Amelia's face.

Things were looking up already.

'No, but he is someone who owes me a favour . . .'

Already published

BACK IN CHARGE
Mariah Greene

A woman in control. Sexy, successful, sure of herself and of what she wants, Andrea King is an ambitious account handler in a top advertising agency. Life seems sweet, as she heads for promotion and enjoys the attentions of her virile young boyfriend.

But strange things are afoot at the agency. A shake-up is ordered, with the key job of Creative Director in the balance. Andrea has her rivals for the post, but when the chance of winning a major new account presents itself, she will go to any lengths to please her client – and herself . . .

0 7515 1276 1

THE DISCIPLINE OF PEARLS
Susan Swann

A mysterious gift, handed to her by a dark and arrogant stranger. Who was he? How did he know so much about her? How did he know her life was crying out for something different? Something . . . exciting, erotic?

The pearl pendant, and the accompanying card bearing an unknown telephone number, propel Marika into a world of uninhibited sexuality, filled with the promise of a desire she had never thought possible. The Discipline of Pearls . . . an exclusive society that speaks to the very core of her sexual being, bringing with it calls to ecstasies she is powerless to ignore, unwilling to resist . . .

0 7515 1277 X

HOTEL APHRODISIA
Dorothy Starr

The luxury hotel of Bouvier Manor nestles near a spring whose mineral water is reputed to have powerful aphrodisiac qualities. Whether this is true or not, Dani Stratton, the hotel's feisty receptionist, finds concentrating on work rather tricky, particularly when the muscularly attractive Mitch is around.

And even as a mysterious consortium threatens to take over the Manor, staff and guests seem quite unable to control their insatiable thirsts . . .

0 7515 1287 7

AROUSING ANNA
Nina Sheridan

Anna had always assumed she was frigid. At least, that's what her husband Paul had always told her – in between telling her to keep still during their weekly fumblings under the covers and playing the field himself during his many business trips.

But one such trip provides the chance that Anna didn't even know she was yearning for. Agreeing to put up a lecturer who is visiting the university where she works, she expects to be host to a dry, elderly academic, and certainly isn't expecting a dashing young Frenchman who immediately speaks to her innermost desires. And, much to her delight and surprise, the vibrant Dominic proves himself able and willing to apply himself to the task of arousing Anna . . .

0 7515 1222 2

THE WOMEN'S CLUB
Vanessa Davies

Sybarites is a health club with a difference. Its owner, Julia Marquis, has introduced a full range of services to guarantee complete satisfaction. For after their saunas and facials the exclusively female members can enjoy an 'intimate' massage from one of the club's expert masseurs.

And now, with the arrival of Grant Delaney, it seems the privileged clientele of the women's club will be getting even better value for their money. This talented masseur can fulfil any woman's erotic dreams.

Except Julia's . . .

0 7515 1343 1

PLAYING THE GAME
Selina Seymour

Kate has had enough. No longer is she prepared to pander to the whims of lovers who don't love her; no longer will she cater for their desires while neglecting her own.

But in reaching this decision Kate makes a startling discovery: the potency of her sexual urge, now given free rein through her willingness to play men at their own game. And it is an urge that doesn't go unnoticed – whether at her chauvinistic City firm, at the château of a new French client, or in performing the duties of a high-class call girl . . .

0 7515 1189 7

A SLAVE TO HIS KISS
Anastasia Dubois

When her twin sister Cassie goes missing in the South of France, Venetia Fellowes knows she must do everything in her power to find her. But in the dusty village of Valazur, where Cassie was last seen, a strange aura of complicity connects those who knew her, heightened by an atmosphere of unrestrained sexuality.

As her fears for Cassie's safety mount, Venetia turns to the one person who might be able to help: the enigmatic Esteban, a study in sexual mystery whose powerful spell demands the ultimate sacrifice . . .

0 7515 1344 X

SATURNALIA
Zara Devereux

Recently widowed, Heather Logan is concerned about her sex-life. Even when married it was plainly unsatisfactory, and now the prospects for sexual fulfilment look decidedly thin.

After consulting a worldly friend, however, Heather takes his advice and checks in to Tostavyn Grange, a private hotel-cum-therapy centre for sexual inhibition. Heather had been warned about their 'unconventional' methods, but after the preliminary session, in which she is brought to a thunderous climax – her first – she is more than willing to complete the course . . .

0 7515 1342 3

DARES
Roxanne Morgan

It began over lunch. Three different women, best friends, decide to spice up their love-lives with a little extra-curricular sex. Shannon is first, accepting the dare of seducing a motorcycle despatch rider – while riding pillion through the streets of London.

The others follow, Nadia and Corey, hesitant at first but soon willing to risk all in the pursuit of new experiences and the heady thrill of trying to out-do each other's increasingly outrageous dares . . .

0 7515 1341 5

SHOPPING AROUND
Mariah Greene

For Karen Taylor, special promotions manager in an upmarket Chelsea department store, choice of product is a luxury she enjoys just as much as her customers.

Richard – virile and vain; Alan – mature and cabinet-minister-sexy; and Maxwell, the androgynous boy supermodel who's fronting her latest campaign. Sooner or later, Karen's going to have to decide between these and others. But when you're shopping around, sampling the goods is half the fun . . .

0 7515 1459 4

INSPIRATION
Stephanie Ash

They were both talented painters, but three years of struggling to make a living from art have taken the edge off Clare's relationship with her boyfriend. The temptation to add a few more colours to her palette seems increasingly attractive – and proves irresistible when she meets the enigmatic and charming Steve.

But their affair is complicated when Steve's beautiful wife asks Clare to paint his portrait as a birthday surprise. Clare is more than happy to suffer for her art – indulging in some passionate studies of her model *and* her client – but when a jealous friend gets involved the situation calls for more intimate inspiration . . .

0 7515 1489 6

DARK SECRET
Marina Anderson

Harriet Radcliffe was bored with her life. At twenty-three, her steady job and safe engagement suddenly seemed very dull. If she was to inject a little excitement into her life, she realised, now was the time to do it.

But the excitement that lay in store was beyond even her wildest ambitions. Answering a job advertisement to assist a world-famous actress, Harriet finds herself plunged into an intense, enclosed world of sexual obsession – playing an unwitting part in a very private drama, but discovering in the process more about her own desires than she had ever dreamed possible . . .

0 7515 1490 X

X Libris offers an eXciting range of quality titles which can be ordered from the following address:

Little, Brown and Company (UK), P.O. Box 11, Falmouth, Cornwall TR10 9EN

Alternatively you may fax your order to the above address.
FAX No. 01326 317444.

Payments can be made as follows: cheque, postal order (payable to Little, Brown and Company) or by credit cards, Visa/Access. Do not send cash or currency. UK customers and B.F.P.O. please allow £1.00 for postage and packing for the first book, plus 50p for the second book, plus 30p for each additional book up to a maximum charge of £3.00 (7 books plus).

Overseas customers including Ireland please allow £2.00 for the first book plus £1.00 for the second book, plus 50p for each additional book.

NAME (Block Letters) _____

_____

ADDRESS _____

_____

_____

☐ I enclose my remittance for _____

☐ I wish to pay by Access/Visa card

Number _____ Card Expiry Date _____